T5-AFS-704

PAUL BUNYAN

of the

Great Lakes

PAUL BUNYAN

of the

Great Lakes

by

STAN NEWTON

**Cover Art: an original oil painting by
Keith Avery**

PAUL BUNYAN

of the

Great Lakes

By Stanley D. Newton

Published
by
Avery Color Studios
AuTrain, Michigan 49806

Library of Congress Card No. 85-70346
ISBN-0-932212-42-5

Printed - February 1985

PAUL BUNYAN OF THE GREAT LAKES was first published in 1946.

To G. Harold and Stewart Earle, founders of the Paul Bunyan Museum, Blaney Park;

To Joe Beach and John Hunter, captains of the Tahquamenon Country;

Last but not least, to a better understanding between the peoples of Russia and the United States.

Acknowledgments

Thanks are due to Professor Earl Clifton Beck, Central Michigan College of Education, for permission to use some of the lumberjack songs and verses in this book; to Pete Vigeant, Sault Ste. Marie, Michigan; William L. Norton, Manistique, Michigan; and Walker Hall, Sault Ste. Marie, Ontario, for help with copy.

The writer is grateful to countless contributors of Paul Bunyan stories to the Bureau News, of which he was for years associate editor. He thanks the Upper Peninsula Development Bureau and Secretary-Manager George E. Bishop and other officers for permission to use many of these cheerful northwoods tales.

Contents

(9)

Cast of Characters

TIME: 1849-1890.

PLACE: The Upper Peninsula of Michigan, sometimes known as the Lake Superior region, or the Land of Hiawatha.

CHARACTERS: *Paul Bunyan*, American-born, of Russian descent, giant logger and lumberman. He logged off the white pine forests of upper Michigan.

Tiny (Finn), Paul's girl, four feet one inch tall, and every inch a beauty.

Sourdough Sam (Norwegian), the camp cook. He fried the sinkers or doughnuts, and

Big Ole, the Swede blacksmith, punched the holes.

Joe Kadunk (Pole), the second cook. He invented blueberry pie.

The Three Hundred Cookees, assistants to Sourdough Sam and Joe Kadunk. They worked 23½ hours a day.

Johnny Inkslinger (Scotch), the camp clerk. A saving man.

Forty Jones (Cornish), the walking boss. He hired 'em without notice and fired 'em the same way.

Chris Crosshaul (Dane), the straw boss or woods foreman, a hound for work.

Bill Half-a-Day (Ojibway Indian), lumberjack cruiser and songster.

One-Eye LaRue (French), the barn boss. He rustled the cat-tail fodder and suckers for Babe's meals.

(11)

Awkward August (Dutch), the camp gardener. His whiskers turned green in the spring.

Truthful Tim (Irish), cookee, camp store-keeper and cobbler.

Sniffy McGurk and thousands of scrappy northern Michigan lumberjack philosophers.

Babe, the Big Blue Ox, and what an ox!

Benny, the off ox. How he loved flapjacks!

Elmer, the world's only Moose Terrier.

Alexander and *Napoleon*, the tomcat champ-ions of the pineries; and other canny dwellers in the green northwoods.

Foreword

Ilya Murometz, hero of Russian folklore, the Ojibway demigod Manibozho, and Paul Bunyan have much in common. The student of Lake Superior Americana finds some curious parallels in the Byliny sagas which still survive in parts of Russia, the tales told around Ojibway Indian campfires, and the yarns spun in many a northern logger's bunkhouse.

The Bunyan epos may well have had its roots in the Russian times of Yermak and Rurik and the early Norseman's invasion of Russian lands in the 9th Century. When the Scandinavian sea kings turned inland and took Novgorod and Kiev, the Viking became the Russian Knaiz. These natural story-tellers merged with the Slavs, but they have left traces of their origin in the Byliny tales.

The hero of superhuman strength and wisdom shines through the Russian chronicles of the 11th and 12th centuries. He dominates the story of Nestor, and the Raid of Prince Igor, who was guided by woodpeckers and was a master of woodcraft. The Fables of Krylof parallel the feats of Paul Bunyan, whose destiny it was to provide housing for the people of the great and growing central west.

It is more than possible that the first Russian immigrant woodsman brought the embryo Paul Bunyan to Maine and New Brunswick. Traveling westward from the Atlantic coast and the Ottawa river, the Bunyan saga received a liberal tincture of Indian tradition from the Ojibways who live along the south shore of Gitche Gumee, Big-Sea-Water, or Lake Superior. Hundreds of Ojibways have followed their natural occupation of woodsmen. For years they have gathered around the sleeping camp stoves with lumberjacks from many lands, and have contributed their share of legend and abounding good humor to the tall tales of the northern forests.

Manibozho, the Great Hare of the Hurons, seems to have grown stronger in Ojibway mythology with the coming of the. Hurons to the land of the mighty lake. Fleeing from the bloodthirsty Iroquois, the remnants of the Huron nation took up their abode in 1653 on the shores of Huron Bay, a rare and beautiful spot on the south shore of Lake Superior in Upper Michigan. Eventually they were absorbed into the Ojibway nation, but the bay, the Huron Mountains and the Huron River still tell of their travail. And so do the wondrous tales of Manibozho.

The Great Hare built the rocky dam in St. Mary's River at Pauwating or Sault Ste. Marie; Paul Bunyan was his white counterpart in raising the Lake Superior water level. The beaver and the porcupine were sacred to Manibozho; Paul warned his lumberjacks never to kill either except in case of dire necessity.

This advice, of course, had an economic foundation. The Ojibway and Ottawa chiefs in the Abinadong River country of Algoma set up a game sanctuary, a forbidden area said to be haunted by windigoes or evil spirits, for miles along the wild river banks. When the inevitable years of famine came, the ban was lifted and the Indians found food and succor in a teeming wild life haven. Hon. Chase S. Osborn, former Governor of Michigan, tells the story in his book, "The Iron Hunter."

Manibozho did tricks with the sun and moon on occasion; Paul Bunyan installed the Northern Lights to provide longer working hours for his logging crews. Manibozho summoned the King of the Fishes with his magic arts; Paul Bunyan rode for miles on the back of a sturgeon. The Ojibway story of the deluge took the form of a relentless snowstorm which threatened to smother every living thing. Paul and his men were bewildered and baffled by the Winter of the Blue Snow.

The resemblances are manifold, and Paul Bunyan, gigantic mortal, was even accorded a supernatural ending by his admirers, in line with his superhuman attributes. He shared the nature not only of Manibozho but of Gitche Manito, Mishosho, Maswein the Manitoulin magician, Mas-kwa the great hunter, the windigoes of the forests and fields, and the Iroquoian Hayawentha whom Longfellow transformed into an Ojibway hero.

Our northern woodsmen, declaring everything grist that comes to their mill, have given us more than gales of laughter in the Lake Superior version of Paul Bunyan. In their modern escape from reality they have materialized a great American saga whose healthy, earthy, woodsy humor can be a potent tonic to a troubled world.

Loafing the happy-go-lucky days away in some tight little log cabin by lake or stream, such as we all dream about but few achieve, many a fine old philosopher ever grows more mellow in the Gitche Gumee woods. These graduates from northern lumber camps—call them shackers if you like—find peace and solace and a grand inner satisfaction in the great Tahquamenon swamp, the Nahma area in Delta County, and other woodland havens in Michigan's Upper Peninsula.

These sages have solved every question of life worth solving. Any slight frustrations in their once-fevered careers have been overcome in the creation and the cherishing of Paul Bunyan, their prideful ideal. In Paul every lumberjack sees himself— glorified, justified, perfected.

Truthful Tim, narrator of these tales, is a composite of many Lake Superior woodsmen—Indians and whites, Cornishmen and Swedes, Finns and Frenchmen—breeds now growing all too few. They were a friendly, fighting, boozing lot of yarn-spinners whom it has been my good fortune to know intimately. Around a redhot stove with them on stormy winter nights; tramping, fishing or just loafing with some wise old shacker, I have achieved a new understanding of lumberjack capacity for sublime and soaring invention.

It is worthy of mention that the only enduring sagas thus far mothered by America—the Paul Bunyan and the Hiawatha tales —are grounded in large part in Michigan's Upper Peninsula (see John Bartlow Martin's "Call It North Country"), and particularly in the Tahquamenon River region.

STAN NEWTON.

Sault Ste. Marie, Michigan.

1

Son of a Worthy Sire

Every Upper Peninsula lumberjack knows that Paul Bunyan was born on the old McNerney farmsite on the east bank of the Tahquamenon River, in Luce County, says Truthful Tim.

Some people say that Paul came with his folks from Russia, and we know that his father, Ivan Bunyan, was born there. Mr. Bunyan was a giant, too, and he exemplified the statements of many writers that Russians are molded on a large scale.

Some of the older lumberjacks said their grandfathers remembered Mr. Bunyan's story of his coming to this country. He said that one day when he was a young man in Russia he climbed a tree during a violent windstorm. Before he got to the top the wind developed into a double hurricane, and soon man and tree went sailing off into space.

After traveling four days at a high altitude, he said, the tree began to drop. When he landed he made a hole 50 miles long and a good many miles wide. He was so tired that he promptly went to sleep, and he had a terrible perspiring nightmare. Years later, explorers and voyageurs found that St. Mary's River, which formerly extended all the way to Whitefish Point, had widened to an expanse of more than 20 miles above the rapids at Sault Sainte Marie. Thereafter that part of the river scooped out by Mr. Bunyan's fall was known as Whitefish Bay.

There is a tradition in the north country that Lake Superior came into being when Paul's father came down with his great Siberian elm. Truthful Tim and his friends don't believe it. They say that while Mr. Bunyan was a large man with a pair of very big feet, he hardly could have kicked out the gigantic basin that is Lake Superior. But he did make Whitefish Bay.

There were and are many Russians in the Lake Superior region, and Ivan Bunyan soon found himself at home in the Tahquamenon River valley, not far from the new bay. Like all the Russians, he became familiar with half a dozen languages, including English, and he soon went to work on a trap line. He had learned trapping in the old country, and the valley was a wild life mecca—abounding in beavers, foxes, bears, minks, fishers, otters, deer and an occasional wolf.

He built the first of many bateaux on the river bank, just below the spot where Hiawatha had fashioned his first birch bark canoe a century before. With other members of the Tahquamenon trapping colony, he toted his furs out to the mouth of the river and thence to Sault Sainte Marie two or three times a year. There he met Seraphina, the robust quarter-breed daughter of the assistant factor who sorted and bought his rich catches of furs and peltries.

Seraphina, the future mother of Paul Bunyan, and Ivan were married at the Sault about a year after their first meeting. In the meantime Ivan built the log house which first stood on what is called the McNerney farm clearing near the mouth of the east branch of the Tahquamenon.

Paul Bunyan was born two years later in May, 1849. He was an only child and it is said that he was of average size at birth. No signs and portents attended his natal day, and there was little indication that he would become a giant in girth and stature. The Indian strain showed a little in Paul's handsome face from the start—in his skin, and eyes, and high cheekbones.

So Paul Bunyan's blood was one-eighth Ojibway, and the interfusion did him nothing but good. The lumberjacks said it helped to put iron into him and to grow a lot of hair on his chest and make a great man of him. They allowed that some Indian blood is good for anybody; and said that if they were Indians they wouldn't be ashamed, but would be mighty proud of it. Tim said that some of his best friends were Indians and that he had always wanted to be an Indian chief with a feather headdress hanging all the way down his back, and buckskin leggings and beaded moccasins. He figured that to be a leader of the ancient Ojibway nation was about the top rank that any man could reach, at least in the western world.

Most of our great men have been born in log cabins, and sometimes right-minded folks have been able to preserve their birthplaces. Paul's first home disappeared long ago, but Captain

Joe Beach is always glad to point out the location to passengers on the river boats PAUL BUNYAN and TAHQUAMENON, when they go down the river with him to visit the big falls. It is near the spot where the strong man Kwasind, friend of Hiawatha, was drowned in the stream after his heroic fight with the otters, as Longfellow tells us in his immortal poem.

Thus Paul Bunyan was an American of Russian and Ojibway descent. There have been endless arguments over his nationality. Hundreds of people have claimed him as a brother Finn or Oddfellow, or at least as a distant relative, and his lumberjacks have never doubted that he was the greatest American who ever lived, as well as the biggest.

Paul's great size has never been equalled, or scientifically explained. A college professor who made his doctorate with a Paul Bunyan thesis has said that Paul may have had an overactive gland, and that this probably caused his tremendous growth. A woman writer thinks that Paul was born under the great star Canopus, and this explanation of his thumping size has appealed to many lumberjacks. It was said, too, that a comet blazed in the northern sky on the night when Paul was born, and that this might account for his giant stature.

You can't make maple flooring from poplar trees, and only class can breed class. Paul's father was a great man, too. If it were not for him upper Michigan might be a Canadian province today. Shortly after Ivan Bunyan arrived there was a sharp border line dispute. The Canadian government claimed the Upper Peninsula of Michigan as its rightful possession. When Ivan heard of this demand he hastened to Washington and made a powerful plea to Congress.

"What will become of us settlers in upper Michigan if you turn us over to Canada?" he asked Congress. "Our northern winters are cold enough now, and it's all we can do to put up with them. We never can stand the Canadian winters. I'm opposed to any such move in the interests of plain common sense. It will surely make our climate colder than ever, to say nothing of the loss to this country of timber and fish, and the fine upstanding Russian men and women I was planning to bring over."

Congress could see that here was a man who knew what he was talking about. It recognized the wisdom of his argument, and the members refused to surrender upper Michigan to Canada. Of course, this happened before Paul Bunyan was born, but it shows the genius of his father Ivan. "Like father, like son" is a true saying, and Paul certainly did his father and mother proud. So Paul almost was born a Canadian, but he was lucky enough to have a father with lots of horse sense. That is why he first met his parents in Northern Michigan instead of in Northern Ontario.

2

The Great Tahquamenon Swamp

Every lumberjack knows, too, says Tim, that this northwoods country is a wonderful land, with big trees, big lakes, and big men everywhere. In the year of Paul Bunyan's birth, five hundred miles of heavy timber covered the south shore of Lake Superior and the north shores of Lake Huron and Lake Michigan; and in these woodlands were rivers, mountains, creeks, springs, lakes and waterfalls in great variety.

It's a fine, healthy country—a made-to-order breeding place for a king among men like Paul Bunyan. This land has given millions of feet of logs and millions of tons of iron and copper ores to the world. Best of all, it gave Paul Bunyan to mankind—Michigan's and Russia's bounty to the Universe.

Paul's birthplace is in the great Tahquamenon swamp near the south shore of Lake Superior. It's a region brimming with romance and history, a wonderful background for a care-free vacation, a land where dozens have spent a happy lifetime.

The Tahquamenon river valley extends from a point north of Seney near Grand Marais, to Whitefish Bay, about one hundred miles away. By no means all of this region is swamp land. Newberry, Eckerman, Strongs, Hulbert and other communities, and parts of Luce, Alger, Schoolcraft and Chippewa counties rise well above the river level on their hardwood clay knolls and ridges of sandy loam. But for the most part the river terrain is an evergreen swamp area, a swamp remarkably different from any other the world over.

Now most people think of a swamp as a stagnant, smelly, snake-infested and generally unpleasant place, remarks Truthful Tim. But if they could see the great Tahquamenon swamp, it would open their eyes. From the center to the edges of these amazing marshes the sweetest waters in the world are found everywhere, bubbling icy-cold from thousands of springs and running off through dozens of sparkling creeks to Lake Superior.

Long stretches of the river are colored a golden tint by the peat beds through which it flows, but there isn't a drop of dirty, stagnant water in the entire area.

It's the same with the Tahquamenon air. All day long the purifying breezes off Hiawatha's Big-Sea-Water blow over and across the swamp, no part of which is very far from the giant lake. The prevailing winds are from the northwest, and they float over the marshes crystal-clear, dustless, and pollen-free; water-washed, and guiltless of human contamination. Frequent rains and abundant snow help to keep the streams moving healthily and the vegetation green and vigorous.

Many white men, locally known as shackers, and hundreds of Ojibway Indians have passed lives of peace, comfort and contentment in the great Tahquamenon swamp. If there ever was a place where folks are free from care, it is that heavenly domain. They call it a swamp, but it really isn't a swamp at all; it's a paradise on Earth, a flower garden, a beautiful park where no one works because no work is necessary there.

Happy living isn't expensive in the Tahquamenon swamp. All one needs is an ax and a box of matches and a cheerful and handy disposition,—and a little Peerless smoking tobacco and snoos, of course. One can build a log shack in no time, and he can cook his meals in the open until he can borrow or steal a camp stove. The folks who live there haven't much of anything, but if they had a million what could they do with it away out there in the swamp?

Think of it! Not a gas station or a traffic light, or a telephone or a bill collector in a thousand square miles! This great Tahquamenon swamp of ours is heaven-come-down-to-Earth, affirms Tim; with its sweet, cool, running water everywhere, and berry patches, and truffle beds; bears in the front yard, deer in the back yard, and wolves and foxes dropping in, friendly-like; a flock of porcupines on the right and a couple of beaver dams on the left; is there anything else that heart could wish for? And not a snake to be seen anywhere!

Millions of dollars in timber have been taken from the great Tahquamenon swamp, and it has yielded untold values in furs over a period of two hundred years. This land has given immense wealth to Michigan, and if it is properly handled and conserved it will grow millions more. Tahquamenon Upper Falls, deep in the heart of the swamp and reached only by a water trip of unrivalled beauty, is a priceless asset and one of the Seven Wonders of upper Michigan.

The food supply has always been abundant in the valley. The meat question, for instance, is no problem at all. The Tahquamenon menu includes deer, bear, rabbits, partridge, prairie chicken, otter, beaver, muskrat and other edible animals. There are a dozen or more varieties of game and pan fish. Blueberries are everywhere in season, and cranberries, strawberries, wild cherries, raspberries and blackberries.

All kinds of garden truck grow luxuriantly. Temporary jobs —not too long or arduous, you understand—are not hard to find; taking care of small needful outlays for clothes, tobacco, snoos and a few groceries. A little snoos is a real aid to clear, calm, deep thinking. When you can have all this for practically nothing, why worry?

"The happiest man I ever knew lived in the Tahquamenon swamp," says Truthful Tim. "He owned a brook."

Here is a place for the cultivation of realistic philosophy. Beyond doubt there is more genuine happiness per capita in the Tahquamenon swamp than there is in Detroit or Cleveland or Chicago. Summer heats are far away. There are no gangsters here, no slums, no blighted areas, no iron pavements, no sweaty, breathless nights. The winters are sharp, but fuel for a thousand years is right at hand. There isn't a single thing to get fussed up over in the whole Tahqamenon domain.

Just imagine that you're living in the great Tahquamenon swamp. If you get tired of staying in one place, moving is no trouble. All you need to do is to wet down the fire and call the dog; then take your ax and matches and snoos, and move. Where else in all the world could you move as easily as that?

So, you see, the Tahquamenon swamp isn't the dark, dismal, creepy place you thought it was. It's alive and sparkling with health and vigor and good cheer, abounding in wild life and flowers and lush vegetation, and it's one of the friendliest and loveliest places in the world.

The grandest feature about the Tahquamenon swamp isn't the big waterfall, although it is a fine spectacle in a unique state park that is reached only by water. Nor is it the meandering river, or the deer, or the fish. The fact that Paul Bunyan was born here, above all makes the swamp outstanding and famous.

3

Paul and the Bobcat

At the age of four years, Tim relates, Paul Bunyan was a lusty youngster weighing eighty pounds and growing rapidly. The cool green woods crowded up to the back door and around his home, and soon he was toddling through the bush and making friends with the deer and the porcupines. Some folks think that he found and ate a magic herb in the forest and that it made a giant of him, but the lumberjacks say that Nature intended him to grow big and strong and that he was no more than fulfilling his destiny.

There is a story that Paul's mother weaned him on Three-Star Hennessey when he was nine months old. But Paul told Tim that he well remembered how she weaned him by giving him maple syrup from the time he was six months old. He said the syrup was made on the farm, and that she fed him a quart of it every daylight hour for a week and more. It was as sweet and palatable as his mother's milk, he said, and he didn't drink any Hennessey until his third year. It's really remarkable how such stories spread when a great career is concerned.

When he was six years old Paul sometimes slept on summer nights in a back yard tent. One evening he ate too many gum-drops, and that night he tossed so much in his sleep that the tent and several acres of standing timber were wrecked. After that when Paul slept out he made his bed in the clearing between the house and the river.

A little later something happened which clearly indicated a great future for Paul. One evening his father, who had been running trap lines down the river, walked into the clearing and found little Paul—he was only six feet tall then—sitting under a tree and chewing the raw ham of a bobcat. The animal had climbed the tree and leaped down on Paul with the idea, perhaps, that the boy would make a tender meal. But Paul saw the bob-cat jump, and caught it in the air and choked it to death. It weighed fifty pounds, and Paul came through without a scratch.

When Paul killed the bobcat his parents realized that their little boy was growing up. They sent him to the nearest school, at Eckerman, thirty miles away through the woods across the Tahquamenon marshes. The daily walk to school and back was fun for Paul. He was three hundred pounds of muscle and sinew and rugged bone.

He learned the alphabet and the multiplication table without trouble, but he loved to play hookey and go roaming through the woods. That was always his idea of a good time. He knew where there was a string of beaver dams, and he often fished for speckled trout with his father and other boys in the good fishing holes, the wide waters above the dams.

He knew that beavers are great travelers, and that when the daddy of a colony gets the wanderlust, he and his brood may turn up fifty miles away. The boy carried home armfuls of cat-tails picked in marshy places, and bouquets for his mother of spiderwort, water plantains and water lilies. He gathered blue flags for her, and pickerel weed, and beautiful wild grasses, or-chids culled from the slimy ooze of creek shores, pitcher plants and wild roses.

Paul was on good terms with a boy named Mike Kallous who lived in the nearby town of Strongs. Mike was a young giant, too. When he was an infant his father had cut off the top of a South Shore railway box car, nailed a handle on it, and gave it to his wife as a baby buggy for Mike. When Mike was eight months old he kicked the sides out of his freight car baby car-riage. His mother threw away the body of the car and gave Mike the car wheels, which he used as teething rings.

Tim said there was a tradition that Mrs. Bunyan gave Paul a couple of blacksmith's anvils for the same purpose when he was a baby. Tim added that he had often seen the anvils but had never been there when Paul was chewing on them. He was a conscientious man and wouldn't make a statement that he couldn't swear to.

One day when Paul and Mike were still young shavers—they could hardly see over the tree tops—they went out to play in the sand on the hillside near Mike's home. They found a couple of shovels, and before they were called in to supper they had piled sand a thousand feet high in the back yard. Then they ran away. Mike's father hired a dozen men, two steam shovels and four or five teams of horses, and the men worked two weeks with this equipment before the yard was cleared.

About this time Ivan Bunyan presented his young son with Elmer, a lively pup that became in later years the world's only moose terrier; and Babe, a young bull giving promise of great size. This made Mike Kallous jealous, and he resolved to find a pet, too, that would be all his own. While in the woods one day he picked up a baby bobcat which he brought home and patiently tamed, naming it Josephine.

Mike fed large amounts of moose milk daily to Josephine, and before long she weighed sixty pounds. The neighbors hated her because she scratched holes in their roofs and destroyed their chimneys. She loved to lie for hours on a roof in the sun. When she smelled the odors of cooked foods she thought it was the chimney that smelled so good, and she bit off the chimney top.

The town marshal warned Mike to keep Josephine tied up, but there wasn't a rope in the village that was strong enough for the purpose. Mike's uncle sent him a forty-foot snake skin from South America, and Mike used it as a leash for Josephine. Mike and Paul were fishing one day in the east branch of the Tahquamenon River. Mike had taken Josephine along and had tied her to a tree near the mouth of Crabapple Creek. Trying to jump across the narrow stream, Josephine fell into the water and drowned.

Mike mourned so deeply for his pet that he went into a decline and died in a few months. His father gave the snake skin to the township, and it proved so strong and tough that it is used as a bridge across Crabapple Creek to this day.

4

They Knew Paul

Paul Bunyan blessed the world with many great inventions. One of his very first was made while he was a schoolboy at Eckerman. Like some other useful discoveries, it was the result of an accident.

Paul's midday meal was put up by his mother, and he carried it to school in a tin pail. It usually consisted of roast moose or deer meat, sliced bread, butter, gravy, a pickle or two and an occasional piece of pie. At noon one day he placed the bucket on his bench, forgot it for a moment, and then sat down on it.

The school kids fished out the bread that wasn't too badly smashed, added more for their own lunch kits, and had a good time eating hamburger sandwiches with Paul. Before long hamburgers became popular all over the north country. It was the fortunate beginning of a great industry.

The boy's size was getting out of all bounds. His father gave him a pair of roller skates. Another boy stole them one night when they were left outside the house, and they were so big that the boy had to steal Babe to haul them home. They were eventually acquired by the owner of a logging railway, and he put flanges on the wheels and used them to haul logs on his road. When the Duluth, South Shore & Atlantic line bought the logger's outfit, Paul's skates were converted into gondola cars. They are still in use, and each of them carries fifty tons of iron ore at one loading from the Ishpeming mines to the ore dock at Marquette.

Paul studied McGuffey's first, second and third readers, writing and arithmetic. Occasionally he played hookey, running away for a day in the woods which were his chief passion. Otherwise he gave the teacher no trouble. He advanced to the fifth grade, and the day came when he could squeeze only with difficulty through the schoolhouse door. Growing so fast, he was out of tune with other boys and girls of his age.

On the afternoon of his last day in school, he was alone with the teacher for a few moments. He hoisted her off the floor in his arms and gave her a farewell kiss. She liked it, so he gave her a half dozen more. They cried a little, and Paul allowed that he was too big for any use. If she thought differently she didn't tell him so, but after all he was only twelve years old. Years later she said that she had the strangest feeling when Paul hugged her, and that her heart went pit-a-pat for hours afterward.

Paul Bunyan was a genius, of course, and a long and formal education wasn't necessary in his case. What is a genius? Isn't it a man who can always find someone to do the dirty work for him? Certainly, says Truthful Tim, and Paul always found somebody like Johnny Inkslinger to attend to petty details while Paul's mind visioned and shaped the great logging and lumbering deals which were hatching in his brain even when he was only a schoolboy at Eckerman.

He loved the woods more than anything else in the world. He often told his lumberjacks that he never could have been anything but a logger or a lumberman. They could see plainly that Nature had intended him for that special job.

The vast Mississippi valley was filling up with settlers, and there was a growing demand for Michigan timber. Prices were going up, and Paul's father found it profitable to do some timber jobbing as well as trapping in the winter seasons. He felled some sizable lots of pine along the Tahquamenon River.

No doubt Paul learned much from his father, but no one taught him the art of logging. He was the man who invented plain and fancy logging and thus made the northwoods famous. After two winters in woods camps Paul easily outdid his father at chopping, hauling, swamping, skidding, decking, loading and all other logging jobs. He said logging was what he was cut out for, and by the holy old Mackinaw he would never let a week go by without finding some new and better way to handle timber.

Ivan Bunyan was proud of his son. He saw clearly that Paul was a genius and that he surely would become the greatest logger of all time. By that time he was nine feet tall and still growing. His father's lumberjacks said he looked high and proud—like an eagle sure of itself. His dark skin had the glint of copper in it, matching well his light brown hair. From the age of 19 or

so he sported a bushy sun-bleached moustache, and his great beak
of a nose loomed above it like the prow of a ship.

His dress was the same as his men's—gray stag pants, high
laced boots, checkered wool shirt in winter and brown cotton in
summer. All of the records say that he was fond of Peerless
eating tobacco and snoos, or snuff.

Sniffy McGurk said that there was always something doing
when Paul Bunyan was around. He didn't wait for something to
happen. He just naturally made things happen. "I've known Paul
since I was knee-high to an eel," he said. "I ate with him and
slept with him and went fishing with him. I've gone in swimming
with him in many a lake and river, and I've borrowed his eating
tobacco dozens of times.

"Paul hated a liar above all things. He often said to us: 'Boys,
whatever you do, always speak the truth. It pays to stick to the
plain unvarnished truth, and anyway you'll be caught if you're
guilty of lying.' That's mighty good advice, and I've never forgotten it."

"When I worked first for Paul Bunyan, I was a cookee in
Sourdough Sam's camp kitchen," says Truthful Tim. "Let me
explain for the benefit of those who are not lucky enough to
have a real lumberjack education, that a cookee is the cook's
helper in a logging camp. Sourdough Sam was the king of the
kitchen, and not even Paul Bunyan could tell him what to do,
except in a crisis. Some of us dreamed of the day when we could
be real camp cooks, too.

"Later on I was a clerk in the camp store, which we called the
van, or the wanigan. Sometimes I cobbled the lumberjacks' boots
there while pursuing my studies for the ministry. I worked for
Paul in the open woods a part of the time, and I knew Big Ole,
the blacksmith, and all the rest of Paul's immortal crew. I propose to tell the honest Paul Bunyan truth about them.

"Paul Bunyan loved the truth with all that big heart of his—
it must have weighed at least 15 pounds, he was so big. He said
it is a shame that so many people tell lies when the truth would
serve their purpose just as well. Of course, lumberjacks are the
squarest and most honorable people in the world, anyway; and
even if there was a liar or maybe two liars in the crew, Paul

was so truthful and set such a good example that they became truthful, too.

"Paul has gone to a higher sphere," continued Tim, "but he has left many reliable witnesses of his great deeds here in northern Michigan—men like Steve Lowney, Dan Sullivan, Bob Blemhuber and others who are just as truthful as I am. They worked for Paul in the pine woods and borrowed his eating tobacco, too. They went fishing with him and helped him log off the pine forests here in the Lake Superior country.

"Then there is Judge Erskine, who lives in Allenville. When he was young he cookeed for Sourdough Sam and Joe Kadunk in Paul's cook camps, and now he's a judge. His life shows how Paul inspired everyone who knew him.

"There are Matt Surrell of Newberry, who swamped for Paul in the eighties; Captain Ben Truedell of Grand Marais, who was a Lima locomotive fireman on Paul's logging railway; and Phil Grondin of Seney, who was manager of Paul Bunyan's Pivot Hotel. It was the world's most remarkable hotel, and there has never been anything like it since.

"Pete Vigeant, who lives in Sault Ste. Marie, will also endorse my statements. He was Johnny Inkslinger's assistant for a while in the camp office. Shortly before Paul passed out, or perhaps I should say up, he gave Pete his watch and chain. Pete keeps them in his safe. They are precious relics of the world's greatest logger, and money can't buy them. Every now and then some millionaire drops around and asks Pete to name his price, but Pete is faithful to Paul's memory and he just can't bear to sell them. We lumberjacks hope that Pete will present them eventually to the Paul Bunyan museum at Blaney Park.

"Of course, you've heard of Doctor Whiteshield of Trout Creek," says Tim. "He was a famous fisherman and the poet laureate of Cloverland, as the Upper Peninsula of Michigan is sometimes called. He recorded Paul Bunyan's doings in verses which speak eloquently of the vast forests, the more than a thousand inland lakes and the hundreds of trout streams in this region.

"Paul's remaining lumberjacks are planning to place a suitable tablet on the spot where he was born, as soon as we can raise the money," concludes Tim. "The old farm on the bank of the Tahquamenon is a location of outstanding historical interest, for Paul Bunyan was born there.

"Hiawatha came into being through the genius of Long-fellow, and there could be no proper understanding and appreciation of Paul Bunyan in the world if there were no lumberjacks. The country and the world owe us lumberjacks more than they can possibly repay, for we have saved for them Paul Bunyan, God's choicest gift to the world."

5

The Thirty-four Devils

Sniffy and Tim were young and care-free in 1869, when they started to work for Paul Bunyan at his camp in the Thirty-Four Hills. Paul took the contract that year to log off this celebrated location in Chippewa County. The area is known as section thirty-four, town forty-seven, north range four east, and it is not far from Rexford.

The boys thought themselves lucky to be working for Sourdough Sam as a couple of the 300 cookees. About 700 lumberjacks were on Paul's payroll in the Thirty-Four Hills that winter, a sizeable crew, but not to be compared with the gangs of later years when he was logging all over the north country.

The new cookees threw their turkeys or pokes, as they were called, in a corner of the cook camp, and went exploring in this little city at the edge of the hills. There were twelve long tables in the eating camp, which was under the same roof as the kitchen. There was room for more than 50 men at each table, and Joe Kadunk, the second cook, told Tim and Sniffy that all hands had breakfast and supper there daily. About 400 hands had their weekday dinners there, too, while the noon meal was toted out to several hundred more in the woods.

The tables were topped with clean, bare white pine boards, and nearly all the dishes were made of tin. Paul Bunyan's big table near the door was covered with plain yellow oilcloth, and the dishes there were larger than the others. The camp walls were built of peeled Norway pine logs, perfectly straight and with no taper from end to end. On them was an occasional sign, SILENCE, or NO TALKING HERE, and a large calendar hung near Paul's table.

The kitchen range was an enormous affair, and the boys wondered how it had been brought to camp. It had been hauled in sections from Rexford, the nearest railway station to the southward. The floors in the kitchen and eating camp had been scrubbed white by the cookees, who were busy with the job of setting the tables and getting dinner ready.

The boys took a quick look over the single street in the camp. West of the dining camp was the office and camp store, or van, sometimes called the wanigan. Paul Bunyan and Johnny Ink-slinger slept there. To the eastward were the two big sleeping camps, while across the driveway and back in the woods a few rods were the stables, blacksmith shop and smaller buildings that might have been warehouses and an icehouse.

Tim and Sniffy were put to work at once by Joe Kadunk in the absence of Sourdough Sam, who was at the Betsey Lake camp until evening. The cookees or cooks' helpers peeled forty or fifty bushels of potatoes daily and set the tables for the lumberjacks' meals. Tim and Sniffy knew what to do without being told, for they had worked in one of Ivan Bunyan's camps down the Tahquamenon.

They helped to keep the food piled high on the tables while the men were eating. They cleared the tables after meals and washed the dishes; they swept the floors, and kept the fires going in the long triple kitchen range and the Quebec stoves in the dining camp, office and store. They fed the pigs and did what-ever other work Sam and Joe told them to do. The immortal three hundred were divided about equally that winter between Camp Thirty-Four and Betsey Lake. One cookee served five or six men at the table, and all of them were busy either in the kitchen or the dining camp at meal time.

Paul Bunyan was the first camp operator to forbid talking at meals. He said talking might start an argument or a fight, and he was right. It often did. So everything was quiet and peaceful when the jacks were surrounding their rations. If one of them wanted food that was out of his reach, he merely nudged his neighbor and pointed at the dish, which was promptly shoved along to him. The less the men talked the more they ate, and how they did eat!

When timber cutting started, Sourdough Sam placed every cookee on a twenty-three and one-half hour daily schedule. There were no labor laws in those days, and the cookees never went to bed from December until April. Sam ordered them to tack a long row of pads on the wall of the cook camp, ear-high from the floor. The only time allowed for sleeping that winter was from 2:30 to 3 o'clock in the morning, when they were permitted to rest their heads on the pads while in a standing position. Their daily tasks began at 3 o'clock, as breakfast for the woods crew had to be prepared and ready at 3:30.

"Many nights I did not sleep at all," says Tim. "I tried to wash and wipe my last pile of dishes before 2:30 o'clock in the morning in order to reach my pad on time, but generally my knees buckled before I was fast asleep, or the first breakfast horn sounded. You might think it was a hard life for us boy cookees, but my health was good and nearly all the cookees gained weight during our first winter in camp.

"Sometimes I ground the kitchen knives for Sourdough Sam," added Tim. "He gave me the job because I was willing and husky. The fact is that I had to be strong to turn the camp grindstone. It was so blamed big that I couldn't turn it all the way around more than two or three times between the monthly paydays."

There was a nickname for everyone in the camp. The lumberjacks called the head cook Sourdough Sam the Stummick Robber. Of course, that was just their little joke, for Sam was a number one cook and he dished up the very best of meals. Sam was a ruddy, fair-haired Norwegian, with a wide mouth which showed several gold teeth when he talked. Six feet tall, he had a commanding air and walked with a slight limp. The camp opinion was that he had been a Norwegian cavalry officer and that he had a past.

Sam's nickname is remembered everywhere in the Lake Superior country to this day. When tourists begin to flock northward in the summer to the Paul Bunyan country, if the table service in the hotels and restaurants isn't satisfactory, they are likely to say: "Well, Sourdough Sam the Stummick Robber must be running this place."

In those days there were no screens on the doors of the camp buildings, and the cook camp especially was plagued with flies. Sourdough Sam had an idea. He sat down one day at a table and drew a plan for Big Ole, the blacksmith. Ole cut out a section of sheet iron that measured three by six feet, and fastened it to the end of a sapling. This provided Sam with a swell combination fly swatter and pancake turner. He became so expert in its use that he could keep six flapjacks in the air and swat the flies on the kitchen table at the same time. The cookees were goggle-eyed at his wonderful skill.

When the fly season ended, Sam laid aside the combination swatter and turner and mixed a little popcorn with his flapjack batter, so that when the cakes were frying they turned themselves over on the griddle. The cookees swore that Sam was the cleverest cook in all the world, and that it was a great privilege to work for him. Any lumberjack can tell you that there aren't any more flapjacks nowadays like Sourdough Sam used to make.

Sam invented the sinker, too, and this work of genius added immensely to his fame. He often fried three thousand sinkers at one time. Some folks call them friedcakes or doughnuts, but the right name, given them by Paul Bunyan himself, is sinkers. At first there were no holes in the sinkers, but one day while he was frying a batch Sam took a pinch of snoos and had a real inspiration. He asked Big Ole to punch a series of trial holes in a bushel or two of sinkers, as a special favor.

Ole found it rather hard to punch the holes in the first few batches of Sam's sinkers because they were so tough and refractory. But Ole had been a cook in Sweden years before he came to this country, and he advised Sam to mix about ten per cent of pure copper with his sinker dough. After that, Ole had no trouble punching the holes.

The improved model was known all over the north country as Sourdough Sam's soft-nosed, non-skid sinker. Ole loved to punch holes in the new style soft-nosed sinkers. He said he could punch such nice smooth holes in them, much cleaner than in the old model sinkers that contained no copper. And so, two or three times a week, Sniffy and Tim and the other cookees toted three or four thousand sinkers over to the camp blacksmith shop in the afternoon, so that Ole could punch the holes and the cookees could rush them to the tables in time for supper.

Tim never forgot his first winter in Camp Thirty-Four. It was the winter of the deep snow which every well posted northerner knows about. The weather was so cold that it was impossible to keep even the cook camp warm. Tim said that, more than once, when he lifted the big coffee pots from the kitchen stove, the coffee froze solid so quickly that the ice in the pots was still warm half an hour later. Lake Superior froze solid all the way down to the lake floor late in the winter. The icehouse crews actually had to blast out the ice for the summer camps, instead of cutting it.

Babe—he was a big ox by that time, but he wasn't blue then—gave the woods crew a lot of trouble that winter. He appeared to be deaf and didn't pay his usual attention to orders. Paul Bunyan had ordered him placed on the log sleigh haul, but the men could hardly manage two round trips a day to the banking grounds, when they should have made at least four trips on the smooth ice roads.

When the warmer winds of spring came, some of the cookees were walking in the woods one Sunday when they heard Paul's voice rolling through the timber: "Giddap, haw, gee around there, you blankety-blank so-and-so!" It stumped them at first, for they knew that neither Paul nor Babe were working; but they decided that Paul's words had been frozen in the cold spell, and were just thawing out. They could see, too, why the boys had thought that Babe had gone deaf.

The snow was terribly deep that winter, and the cookees dug holes almost daily in the drifts, to keep the smoke pipe clear on the cook camp roof. At one time there was a big hole in the snow nearly a hundred feet deep above the pipe.

When the snow went off in the spring, Babe acted like a surly bucking mustang and refused to haul any more logs on the woods roads. At first Paul thought that Babe hadn't been getting enough to eat, and he talked things over with One-Eye LaRue, the barn boss, and Chris Crosshaul, the woods boss. One-Eye took Paul out to the barn and showed him bin after bin full of cattail fodder. He said that Babe had been fed all he wanted of his favorite ration.

Paul took a pinch or two of snoos and did some hard thinking. Then he had an idea. He felt sure that since Babe had been used to hauling logs only on roads that were white with snow and ice, it would be necessary to put one over on him. So Paul ordered the woods gang to whitewash the roads, and when this was done Babe went to work with a will.

About that time One-Eye LaRue brought a cow to the camp. Her name was Lucy, and she gave down so much milk that a dozen cookees were kept busy skimming it. One time Lucy wandered into a swamp and ate her fill of evergreen boughs. For two weeks after that her milk was so strong that the lumberjacks used it for cough medicine and liniment.

The cookees and Sourdough Sam made tons of butter from Lucy's milk, and one day Sam had a bright idea. Babe was hauling in a couple of big logs at a time with chains attached to his harness. Why not butter the roads and make the slipping better, and use the sleighs all summer? Paul thought it was a grand scheme, and he ordered the woods gang to spread Lucy's butter, uncolored of course, on ten miles of the whitewashed roads as a trial test. This worked so well that all the woods roads were buttered thereafter. Babe's teamsters kept their sleighs in use throughout the summer, and they hauled bigger loads of logs than they had ever been able to handle on the winter roads.

Then One-Eye brought down an extra ox named Benny from the Bodi Lake camp. The woods crew used him as Babe's yoke-mate on some of the log hauls, but of course he was much smaller than Babe. Benny was always hungry, and he was especially fond of flapjacks or belly shingles, as the boys sometimes called the stacks of pancakes fried each morning by Sourdough Sam.

One-Eye forgot to feed Benny one night, and early next morning Benny broke out of his stall and rushed headlong into the cook camp. It was breakfast time, and Benny drove all of the help, cooks and cookees, out of doors and seized and devoured a big pile of Sourdough Sam's flapjacks. When the boys ventured in, Benny rolled his eyes, lowered his big head, and shook it viciously.

At this crisis Sam hatched what he thought was a grand idea. Maybe, he said, if they stole in quietly and fried another stack of flapjacks for Benny, they could pacify him and get him under control. So they pussy-footed into the kitchen, poked up the fire, and fried a couple of thousand flapjacks for Benny as soon as they could. They kept the stove between themselves and

Benny, and he stood glaring at them with his tongue hanging out and foam on his lips, and pawing the floor like mad.

Several dozen cookees stood their ground like men and shoveled flapjacks down Benny's throat as fast as Sourdough Sam and Joe Kadunk could fry them, while Benny reared to the rafters and bellowed for more. The cookees did their level best, but the cooks just couldn't mix the batter and fry the flapjacks fast enough. Rampant and clamorous, Benny seized a big section of the redhot stove in his hungry jaws and swallowed it. In no time he was throwing flip-flops all over the kitchen while the crew went out through the windows.

Some one summoned Paul Bunyan, and he came on the run with a fire extinguisher. He tried to put Benny out, but poor Benny was too far gone. He curled up in a corner of the kitchen, which was practically a total loss, and died there. The crew recovered the stove when it cooled off, and served up the edible parts of Benny for supper next day.

They buried the rest of him in a mound which now is the highest one of the Thirty-Four Hills.

While digging Benny's grave the lumberjacks found the first indications of the great natural snoos vein whose discovery electrified the land. Long after, when the panic of '73 was at its worst, Paul Bunyan developed this deposit and shipped carloads of snoos to all parts of the country. His courage and vision were primary factors in breaking the back of the depression and putting America on its feet again.

6

The Cold Winter of '69

The winter of 1869 was about the coldest ever known in the north country. Tim said that much of the time he had a sore throat from eating food that came to the table piping hot, but which froze hard before he could swallow it.

One morning Sniffy McGurk carried out a pail of boiling water to pour on the stone while grinding his ax. The water froze solid immediately, and the ice was so hot that Sniffy couldn't touch it for a long time.

The temperature went down to 90 degrees below zero, and woods operations ceased until the weather warmed to 60 below, after a week or two. At 50 degrees below the mercury froze in the big thermometer on the outside wall of the office, and for a while Johnny Inkslinger kept the weather tally with a spirit gauge. At 90 below the ax bits snapped when the men tried to chop trees with them, and if a man touched metal with his bare skin, he suffered a severe frostburn.

When woods cutting and hauling were halted by the cold weather, the lumberjacks and their boss went hunting for moose. Tim tagged along behind Paul and Chris Crosshaul one morning in the woods, when it was so cold that their breath turned to icicles the moment it left their mouths. They sighted a moose on a runway, and Paul fired a pailful of bullets at it from his 27-pound field piece. The hunters saw the bullets freeze in the air an instant after they left Paul's gun, and then disappear. He said it was useless to try hunting moose under any such conditions, so the three returned to camp.

Two days later the alcohol thermometer rose from 110 degrees below zero to 40 below. About nine in the morning, when the sun was coming up, the woods gang sent word to camp that someone was shooting at them and that something should be done about it right away. Johnny Inkslinger hurried out on the ice road to the cuttings, where the boys told him that bullets had been zag-zagging in all directions, and they showed him the marks on more than one big pine.

They found Paul's moose dead beside a runway. When the weather warmed up, some of the bullets must have followed the animal and knocked it over. So Paul bagged his moose after all, long after he had given up all hope of getting it.

On one of the very cold winter afternoons when the crew wasn't working, Sourdough Sam stepped to the door of the cook camp and blew the camp horn four times. The men came trooping in for supper from the sleeping camp—they called it the bunk club—and the blares froze quickly and drifted away on the frosty air.

Next morning the weather moderated to about 45 below zero, and the blares thawed out. The woods crew going to work at daylight fell in with four moose herds. The animals had gathered around the blares, which were wailing like flocks of devils with the pip. The moose seemed to be fascinated. They pawed the snow and bellowed and snorted, and never noticed the lumberjacks.

The men ran back to camp for their guns, and they bagged forty-five moose that morning. Babe hauled the carcasses into camp, and when the men left the spot, the blares were still blaring.

All hands were equipped with snowshoes, and the men came and went over the deep drifts without trouble. One day the loading crew broke the old jammer span at the landing, where the long slanting and swinging stick of timber was used to lift the logs from the sleighs to the banking grounds. Paul selected a likely Norway pine tree and ordered the crew to cut and trim a 300-foot jammer arm from it. The men had to work on top of the snowdrifts, and the snow was so deep that later, when it melted and the ground was bare, the stump of the big Norway stood four 16-foot logs high in the air.

The northern Indians call January the snow month and February the cold month. The cook camp simply couldn't be kept warm that February. One morning Sourdough Sam poached the usual five crates of eggs for breakfast. The fire in the kitchen stove was a hot one, but the eggs came to the tables cooked on the bottoms and with the tops solidly frozen.

About that time Sam took to his bed with a cold, in his little room off the kitchen. Joe Kadunk, the second cook, was attending a Polish convention in Milwaukee. Paul called in one of the lumberjacks as a substitute. The man had been a complete failure at all other work given him, so Paul was sure that he must be a cook.

The new man filled the big kettle to the top with navy beans, which showed how much he knew about cooking beans. He added water and poked the fire, and turned to other matters. Soon the beans began to swell, and the cookees lost no time getting out of the kitchen. The beans kept right on swelling until they lifted off the roof and bulged the cook camp walls.

It was a real crisis, and every man that could be spared was rushed to the scene. All hands pitched in and ate beans without stopping for three days and nights before reaching and rescuing the substitute cook and Sourdough Sam, who had been asleep in his bunk when the beans began to swell. Sam said it was the closest shave he ever had, and Tim remarked that since that time he hasn't really cared much for beans.

Sam was eternally grateful to the cookees and lumberjacks who saved his life by eating beans. He said they had done a great service not only to him but to the country. He cooked for Paul Bunyan and his crews many years after that, and of course he was the chef in the famous Pivot Hotel.

Sam was particularly proud of his flapjack batter. He said that he had a secret batter recipe that he could sell for five thousand dollars any day—that he had a standing offer but wasn't interested. His flapjacks were certainly wonderful, said Paul's lumberjacks.

One winter Paul operated a camp on Screw Auger Creek, with a crew of two thousand lumberjacks. That meant batter for forty thousand flapjacks every morning. Paul often said that he had no use for a man that couldn't surround at least twenty flapjacks at a meal; he said a man that couldn't do that much for his country would never make a real lumberjack.

Paul ate as many as forty flapjacks at a meal, and every flapjack was fried on a special griddle nine feet in diameter. There wasn't room enough in the small Screw Auger camp to make a large flapjack batter mix, so Sam mixed his batter in a tank up under the roof of the sleeping camp. Cookees carried the batter and its ingredients up and down a couple of ladders. One warm night the stuff rose suddenly under the tarpaper roof, overflowed the tank, and nearly drowned a dozen men in their bunks just below. Paul's office was in that end of the building and he was asleep there at the time. Smeared with flapjack batter from top to toe, he rushed blindly out of the building and hollered for help. The boys peeled ten barrels of it out of his whiskers.

Sourdough Sam's invention of the soft-nosed non-skid sinker brought him great renown. He was in demand as a speaker—when he could get away—at chefs' clubs and association meetings, and he was presented with medals and diplomas in honor of his genius. He was fond of saying that you can call a sinker a doughnut if you don't mind being out of date, but it's always a sinker for folks that want to have things right and proper.

No one ever heard of a sinker until Sam's brains and vision bestowed it on a grateful world. The sinker was a novelty, it generally tasted good, and the lumberjacks weren't too critical if a batch happened to go a little sour now and then. Its inventor carried his honors with becoming dignity and modesty, realizing full well that he was a benefactor of the human race.

Big Ole, the camp blacksmith, punched the sinker holes in a most workmanlike manner. When he punched the holes in the extra large size sinkers made for Paul Bunyan's table, Ole used a steel punch six inches in diameter, and he drove it through the sinkers with a 40-pound maul. Folks came miles and miles to see Ole punch the holes in Sam's non-skid sinkers, and Ole became famous, too.

Paul's keen intelligence soon discovered that Sourdough Sam's friedcakes, as they were called at first, made excellent sinkers when fastened to a 20-ply line and dropped into Lake Superior, where the big Mackinaw trout lay in wait.

The fish thought the sinkers were bait, but generally they

couldn't make a dent in them. The more the trout tried to nibble the quicker they were hooked. This explains why friedcakes are called sinkers now. That is the modern and correct name given them by folks who try to have everything, including names, right and proper.

7

The Seven Ax-men

In the first winter that Tim worked for Sourdough Sam in the cook camp, Paul Bunyan named the seven best tree choppers in the woods gang and gave each man a gold medal. From that hour they were known to the world as Paul's Seven Ax-Men.

Their skill was unbelievable. One morning they began cutting down trees at Manistique on the north shore of Lake Michigan. They worked all day in virgin timber, chopping down pines measuring four feet or more in diameter at the butt. When night came they had cut a straight clean swath more than a mile wide, through the woods all the way to Munising Bay and Lake Superior, seventy miles across the Upper Peninsula of Michigan from shore to shore. Today state highway M-94 follows the line of their cutting.

The Seven Ax-Men sometimes staged a thrilling ax dance for the lumberjacks, generally in front of the sleeping camp. All seven danced shoulder to shoulder, then turned like a flash and swung their axes at each other, each man ducking just in time to keep his head and trunk together. They were paired off like gladiators, three against three, with Swede Mickelson standing aside and resting on his shining ax like Thor himself, and fought to the death—almost. How their axes whistled and rang as they glanced, and shot great showers of sparks! Tim never could understand how they missed splitting each other in two.

The Ax-Men never sharpened their axes on the big camp grindstone. They climbed to the hilltops, then knocked huge rocks loose and rolled them down. The boulders bounced downward at a terrific clip, while the Ax-Men raced alongside and held the edges of their axes against the whirling stones. When they reached the bottom every ax was so sharp that the owner could shave with it. The Seven Ax-Men always shaved with their axes on Saturday nights or after pay days, when they were going out to town.

In those days the Thirty-Four Hills were much steeper and higher than they are now. One hill was shaped like a pyramid, with a peak so high that some of the lumberjacks required nearly a week to see the top of it. Other lumberjacks couldn't see the summit at all from the bottom of the hill, no matter how hard they tried. Sometimes two men had to look together in order to see the top.

This hill had an area of about 40 acres, and the men called it the Pyramid Forty. A large part of the crew worked all winter on the hill timber, and in the spring three dozen lumberjacks reported one leg five or six inches shorter than the other. The condition was caused by working on the sides of the hill. It was midsummer before their legs returned to normal.

After Benny's dramatic end, Babe, the Big Blue Ox, did the heavy timber hauling without a mate. He didn't need a yoke-fellow, for he was growing steadily on his chosen diet of cat-tail fodder, and he reached gigantic stature. Big Ole, the blacksmith, made a single yoke for him, and although it weighed a ton Babe carried it with ease.

Deer were plentiful in the camp area that winter, and some of the lumberjacks were expert deer hide tanners. Ole cut, bolted and fitted a harness for Babe which he made from the hides of sixty bucks. This immensely tough harness worked well in cold weather, but when the rainy days of spring came the wet harness stretched so much that Babe sometimes arrived at the landing when his load of logs was half a mile behind him in the woods.

This was a real problem at first, but Ole and Chris Crosshaul, the woods foreman, solved it neatly. They went into conference, swapping snuff boxes and doing some deep thinking. They unharnessed Babe at the landing and threw the breast collar over a stump. To keep Babe busy on rainy days they made several sets of buckskin harness for his use, using one harness and one stump to each load. When the sun came out the traces shrank and drew the loaded log sleighs right up to the landing. After that there was no trouble with hauling operations in wet weather. The lumberjacks admired the solution and agreed that there's a way out of every difficulty if folks will only use their heads.

The story of the giant ox's strength is confirmed by later happenings in the Ontonagon valley when he had arrived at full maturity. The season was late, and Paul, chafing at delays, ordered Chris Crosshaul to hook Babe to an entire section of timber and haul it to the banking ground. A section, as you may know, is one square mile.

Chris backed Babe up to the section and hooked on the largest and longest logging chain in the camp. Babe braced himself, grunted, and moved off with the entire section on the other end of the chain. Before he had gone ten rods the chain stretched into a semi-rigid bar of steel. The extreme tension made the links so hot that they welded perfectly. That's how strong Babe was in his prime.

Logging the Thirty-Four Hills in late winter, the crew made slow progress. The snow was deep, felling timber on the steep slopes was a slippery job, and they failed to get out the volume of logs that Paul's contract called for.

He called Chris Crosshaul and Johnny Inkslinger into conference, and with much snuff dipping and hard thinking they worked out a new time table for camp use. Paul ordered Johnny to open another set of books and a new payroll, and he installed three ten-hour shifts of the woods chopping and hauling crews. For a while the woods crews worked nearly as hard as the cookees did.

Paul proved his genius supreme when he solved the night work problem for his men. With Johnny Inkslinger as adviser he invented the Northern Lights. With their help the night crews turned in nearly as many logs as the day crews did, especially when the mercury was down to forty degrees below zero or colder.

The Northern Lights were probably the greatest of Paul's inventions, and while he never did succeed in making them work steadily and perfectly, they did help materially to bring the camp output up to contract that winter. He tinkered with them for weeks, and found in the end that their usefulness depended in great measure upon the weather. The Northern Lights, it seemed, were not just the thing for late night work in summer logging camps. He finally abandoned the project and left the Lights to their fitful flickerings. Oldtime lumberjacks say they've never shone as brightly since. But if you could have seen them in the winter of '69 you would have said they were far and away the grandest sight in the fair north country.

Now Paul Bunyan was a determined man, and he refused to acknowledge defeat when the Northern Lights failed to give him adequate service. He summoned Chris and Johnny to another meeting. There had been some difficulties about the plans for three ten-hour work shifts, but after profound study and figuring they perfected a thirty-hour clock that solved the problem of three shifts a day.

The 300 cookees sat tight and sawed wood, as the saying goes in the Lake Superior forests, but some of them thought that the woods crews really had been working hard enough before the thirty-hour plan was adopted. At one time four crews were busy on the woods cutting and hauling jobs—one working, one going to work, one coming from work, and one eating. It was the finest example of thorough-going efficiency that the north country ever saw.

And still Paul wasn't satisfied. He swore that the timber delivery contract must be filled on time. Paul seldom made a mistake, but he did stub his toe when he ordered the sun to keep time with his new clock. The proudest, most important and most efficient body of men in the world—Paul's lumberjacks—went along with him shoulder to shoulder and obeyed him to the letter; and didn't the mightiest ox in the world do his bidding? After all, wasn't there a little consistency in Paul's idea that even the sun would break with the past and go along with him, too?

But the sun refused to alter its tranquil course by so much as a second. It set its face resolutely against Paul's thirty-hour clock, but Paul was adamant, too. He ordered Johnny Inkslinger to alter the multiplication table in such a way that three times ten would be twenty-four. Johnny, who had been a lawyer and a college professor before he advanced to the post of office manager for Paul Bunyan, worked this out neatly and scientifically. His system was in use for more than two years in the Lake Superior region. However, there were endless complaints from old fogies, and after that the multiplication table was restored to its original form by a special Act of Congress.

Paul knew that Congress would have the law on him if he didn't abide by its decision, so he went back to the regulation twenty-four hour clock, and asked the lumberjacks to work sixteen hours a day. Big Ole was heartily in favor of this ruling. He said:

"By yiminy, Meester Bunyan hay bane da best boss Aye effer vork for. Hay giffus saxteen hours to do day's vork in, and all my udder bosses day bane giffus only tvelve."

This explains why Swedes the world over get fighting mad when they are asked to accept sixteen hours' pay for eight hours' work.

It was in '69 and '70 that Paul Bunyan straightened and improved the first Upper Peninsula roads. Originally most of them were nothing but trails and tote roads through the dense northern woods, made in a hurry and without detailed planning by Paul's swamping crews. Some of these bush roads were so crooked that Paul's teamsters could haul only crooked logs over them at first. When the men began to handle long straight white pine logs, the timber was jammed and tangled on the curves, causing many delays.

Paul solved the problem by hitching Babe to the ends of one crooked road after another and yanking them straight as a beeline. One of Paul's crookedest logging roads is now state highway M-28. It runs thirty miles from Seney to Shingleton through Schoolcraft and Alger counties. Today there isn't a kink, crook, curve or corner in the entire thirty miles, thanks to Paul's genius and Babe's mighty pulling powers.

Michigan state highway officials have always been grateful to Paul Bunyan for his foresight in handling the Upper Peninsula road problem. They say that the State owes a great debt to Paul for building the roads in the first place, and then straightening them with the help of Babe, the Big Blue Ox.

8

A Powerful Man

Nobody claims that an ordinary man can easily tote a sixteen-foot log from a tree that has been flourishing in the woods for three centuries.

Near the state bank in Newberry there is a big white pine log that Paul Bunyan toted into town on his shoulder, about the time he was through logging in Luce county. The records show that the exact time this huge log was brought in by Paul was Wednesday afternoon, June 1, 1888, at 4 p.m. He said he wanted his Newberry friends to have a real virgin white pine log as a keepsake from him; that the pines were going at a great rate and that this log would be his monument in a town where he had always felt at home.

Paul toted this log into town from his Deer Park camp as easily as another man could handle a toothpick. It laid alongside the bank building for a few months after Paul went away. When the grateful officials and citizens of Newberry saw that Paul wasn't coming back, they mounted the log under a canopy on the boulevard. They bound it carefully with strong wire and shellacked the ends, with a view to making the log a perpetual Paul Bunyan memorial.

Now if anyone doubts this, the next time he is in Newberry he can ask Matt Surrell, or Charley Knutson, or Dan McLeod—no, not Dan, he has passed on, and a fine man he was; he learned the art of logging from Paul—and these gentlemen will be glad to confirm the above. Fred Larson owned part of the front and back bars from Paul's Pivot Hotel, a wonderful institution and the largest hotel in the world, and they are now on view in the Luce Hotel at Newberry.

When Paul went out of the hotel business he sold the bar in sections, and Gus Jaeger bought one section. The original bar was more than a thousand feet long, and there wasn't another building in the State of Michigan or the whole northwest big enough to hold it when Paul dismantled the Pivot Hotel.

Gus sold the bar to Tom Moore, and Tom sold it to Jack Johnson. When Jack moved away he sold the bar to Ollie Smith in Trout Lake. The Trout Lake Hotel burned down one night, but Ollie saved the bar and sold it to Dinnie Stites in Gould City. It was too big for Dinnie's place, so he sold it for a song to John Hunt in Newberry, and John presented it to Free Chesbrough.

Free ran a very fine temperance house over in Emerson, where he had a big sawmill. He had no particular use for a bar, and he traded it to Norway Jack for a catch of brook trout. Jack owed Fred Larson a board bill, so he turned over the bar to Fred on account.

When the bar came to Fred he set it up—what there was left of it—in the Luce Hotel in Newberry. Today the boys play smear and tiddly-winks on its solid walnut top, and drink their grape pop over it, and they never dream, or they have long forgotten that it was once the pride of Paul Bunyan's celebrated Pivot Hotel down the Tahquamenon River. But there it is, in downtown Newberry, and there, too, is the Paul Bunyan log, for all the world to see and to admire.

One upon a time Paul signed a contract to log off seven sections of spruce near the mouth of the Hinky Dink River in Schoolcraft County. The contract called for delivery in thirty days, and everybody said that Paul had make a mistake in taking the contract, and that he never could fill it in the world.

But Paul fooled them. He ordered Big Ole to make a wood scythe for him with a blade sixty-two feet long. When Paul got into action with that scythe he cut more timber every hour than the Seven Ax-Men felled in a week. Every time he swung it in a stand of spruce he cut pulpwod enough for paper to print the Escanaba Daily Press or the Sault Ste. Marie Evening News from now until July, 1999. And when the Munising Paper Company's mill had worked up the pulpwood into bond paper, Paul reserved the entire output for Johnny Inkslinger's use in figuring up the monthly camp time sheets and pay rolls.

The north country saying, "Let's kiss the baby," was first used by Paul Bunyan. Maybe you've heard some one say it, with no baby in sight. It's done this way. You walk up to the bar, the bartender sets out a bottle of Three-Star Hennessey and you fill your glass with it. Then you crook your elbow and down the hatch goes the Hennessey, and you take a long look through the bottom of the glass before setting it down. You've kissed the baby.

Paul was not only the biggest man but he was the best man in the woods. He could travel through heavy bush at twelve or fifteen miles an hour, and none of his men could keep up with him. When you consider the trees and stumps and windfalls that a woodsman must dodge, to say nothing of bears and porcupines, when he is striking out through the forests across country, twelve miles an hour is moving right along.

It was worth going miles to see Paul pace off a section line to a section corner in the woods. He never made a mistake. When he was land looking or getting ready for a new logging job, he would pace off the right number of steps—seventeen feet to every pace—dig in his heel, and then tell the crew, when it caught up with him, to drive the stake right there. And when the wood stake was driven down, it always hit the top of the iron stake which had been planted there by government surveyors years and years before, and which had been covered over by falling leaves, humus and dirt.

Once a lumberjack drove a stake at the exact spot picked by Paul, but he failed to strike anything. Paul was surprised. He tore up the earth with his big shovel and found the original surveyor had laid down a grindstone for a marker instead of the usual iron stake. The wood stake had been driven through the hole in the stone. Things like that proved that Paul never had an equal in running lines through the woods.

Paul was never snooty. He was too great a man for that, and when he was out in the bush he dressed as plainly as any of his men. But when he went to see Tiny, his pretty Finn girl who lived in Germfask, he always put some rose-scented vaseline or bear's oil on his whiskers, threw away his eating tobacco, and sweetened his breath with spruce gum.

One evening just before reaching Tiny's home in Germfask, Paul parked his spruce gum on a log beside the old tote road, and when he left he forgot all about the wad he had left behind.

Years later the road was covered with bush, and Jens Jensen, who owned a farm nearby, was out on the old right-of-way looking for a lost heifer. He found her, and two others that were lost the year before, embalmed in Paul's big bite of spruce gum.

Jens hunted up an ax, went back and split the wad open. He found nine deer skeletons, seventeen porcupines, two pecks of pollywogs and a doodad bird, all swallowed up in that mouthful of chewing gum. Jens is building an automobile road to the location and he expects to make a fortune by charging tourists ten cents a look at the biggest cud of gum ever chewed by a human being. Such a remarkable exhibit really belongs in the Paul Bunyan Free Museum at Blaney Park. There it could be seen and marveled at by thousands, demonstrating to any reasonable person that Paul Bunyan was a real big man.

9

Paul's Gallstone Operation

"Certain statements made by me, regarding Paul Bunyan and his great work of logging off the Upper Peninsula of Michigan, have been questioned," says Truthful Tim. "No one claims that I lied, but some folks have insinuated that I have been stretching the truth a little. One man from Cleveland actually said that he didn't believe there ever was such a man as Paul Bunyan.

"I have mentioned several authentic relics of Paul Bunyan that are now on view in the Upper Peninsula, such as the Newberry white pine log, Paul's watch and chain, and others. I am going to give further proofs in this chapter. Paul always said that no matter what happens, the public is entitled to the facts, and those are my sentiments, too. I propose to give plain facts in this chapter, in order that the reader may understand once for all that I never stretch the truth.

"There comes to mind the winter when we logged a large tract of pine near Mustard Pie Lake in Alger county. Paul wasn't well that winter, and his appetite was so poor that he ate only five meals a day, whereas when he was in good health he never ate less than seven or eight. Of course, everybody understands that a man of Paul's huge size has to eat a number of hearty meals daily in order to keep up his strength.

"Paul lost his appetite and he suffered with a pain in his side. To tell the truth our camp meals were below average quality that winter. We had a large supply of navy beans, which were always good when properly cooked, but in saving Sourdough Sam's life in an over-beaned cook camp, I had lost my zest for baked and boiled beans.

"There were good reserves of red horse, which is the lumberjack's name for corned beef made from old dried up critters good for nothing but a logging camp table. There was bread but no butter, so we spread lard on the bread and it didn't taste too bad. There was sowbelly, too. Everybody knows that no woods camp can be run successfully without sowbelly. Sourdough Sam made some nice batches of sinkers every few days, and another product which he called apple sauce. But it wasn't the apple sauce which you and I know and like so well.

"Sam's apple sauce was made of home dried apples. The downstate farmer who owned an orchard harvested his apples in the fall, cut them into thick slices and strung them on cords with a canvas needle or a darning needle.

"His wife dried the strings over the kitchen stove and hung them from the garret rafters for winter use. If there was a surplus he traded the apples for groceries at his store. The storekeeper sold them, packed in barrels, to logger camp supply houses.

"Sam stewed the dried apples in black-strap molasses, which we lumberjacks called treacle. The sauce was so black that it discolored our teeth. The cookees served pans of the stuff which were left on the table until it was consumed. The flies liked it, but sometimes the sauce turned sour and worked and bubbled, killing the flies that ate it. I didn't care for apple sauce but Paul thought it was grand food.

"The cookees had it all figured out that Paul's belly pains were caused by eating too much apple sauce. The pangs grew worse instead of better, and soon Johnny Inkslinger turned the camp books over to me, and then hurried Paul out to the railway and went with him to a Minnesota clinic. The doctors examined Paul and said that he must have an immediate gall bladder operation.

"The country's medical journals gave pages to Paul's operation, and stated that it was one of the most interesting in the annals of medicine. Paul was so big that the doctors had to make dozens of special plans for his reception and treatment.

"Not a hospital in the city was large enough to accommodate Paul, so he had his operation under a circus tent in the park near the river. Half a ton of blasting powder, about a mile of fuse and a big dipper dredge were used on the job. Twenty-five of the clinic's best surgeons took part, and Johnny was on hand for the entire proceedings. He said he stood by Paul throughout the ordeal, and that it was the most thrilling experience of his life.

"First, he said, forty-one barbers went through the preliminaries. Each of them could shave with either right or left hands, and each carried two razors. The attendants pulled Paul's shirt off over his head, and the barbers, working at top speed, shaved his belly in eleven and a half minutes. Thirty-five men were assigned to the grindstones, and they sharpened the surgeon's knives and dipper teeth. One-half of the city's nurses fanned Paul's brow, and the other half practically drained the river dry, they put so many wet towels on his head.

"Johnny said that a railway tank car loaded with chloroform was required for anesthetizing Paul. As soon as Paul was in dreamland the doctors attached a hose to the nearby railway water tank, which had been filled with fly-tox, and they sprayed his stomach over and over. When all was ready they advanced to the attack and sank a shaft southeast of Paul's solar plexus, or maybe it was southwest,—Johnny couldn't remember which, as he had been so excited.

"After the doctors had drilled and blasted nearly two hours, they mined two hundred and thirty-three gallstones out of Paul's bay window. Five of these stones weighed more than five hundred pounds each. The doctors used the dipper dredge and a derrick when they hoisted out the larger stones. Johnny said the entire operation and all the well considered details were the most remarkable examples of medical skill that he ever heard of.

"The operation was a complete success, and before long Paul was up and around. One of the first things he did after recovering was to place two of the smaller stones, weighing about one hundred pounds each, on the gateposts of the greenhouse at the city's edge. These stones may be seen there by any miserable doubter who dares to sneer at the annals of Paul Bunyan. There they stand to this day, shining proof of Paul's gallstone operation.

"They should convince the rankest skeptic who still will not listen to reason. Any number of local people will certify that every statement made here is an honest northern Michigan fact, and they will gladly take scoffers to the spot and point out the gallstones which still adorn the gateposts.

"Paul shipped one of the stones to a jeweler who carved a

beautiful watch charm from it. The jeweler mounted two other stones in a pair of ear-rings which Paul presented to Tiny when he returned to the Upper Peninsula. She said he couldn't have pleased her more. He turned over the rest of the stones to the Minnesota state highway department. The stones were crushed and used for road material, and this was the beginning of the good roads system in the great State of Minnesota.

"Paul kept six stones and eventually gave them to his friend Henry Hossack at Cedarville. Henry was building the Cedar Inn at the time, and he placed those ornamental stones on the wall in front of the hotel. They weigh about forty pounds each and they constitute one of the most remarkable sights of the north country. Lots of Paul's admirers photograph them and send the prints home to their folks. It is said that Paul carried them over to Cedarville either in his grip or his pants pocket.

"These relics of a great man demonstrate to the world that Paul Bunyan really did live here and that he underwent a serious operation. So when you hear some persons bragging about their puny little gallstone operations, don't forget to tell them about the honest-to-Mike gallstones which the doctors blasted out of Paul Bunyan.

"We have many other relics and mementos of Paul, if you want further proof," continued Tim. "Paul's watch and chain may be seen at Pete Vigeant's curio store in Sault Ste. Marie. The watch is seven inches in diameter and its weight is four pounds. The chain is so heavy that some folks have jumped to the conclusion that it was used to anchor a bear trap, but we lumberjacks recall its glorious spread across Paul's Sunday vest. Paul gave Pete a penknife, too. It is a foot and a half long. Paul formerly carried the knife in his vest pocket and trimmed his fingernails with it. I never heard whether he used to it trim his toe nails, but probably he did.

"Paul's fiddle is now the property of a gentleman named Bridgewood who lives in Sebastopol, California. When Babe stayed out in the woods too long while looking for the cat-tails or suckers which were his favorite foods, Paul brought him trotting back to camp in a hurry by playing the fiddle in the open. Paul wrote a song for Babe called 'Buy Low, Bab-ey,' and he could make Babe cry like a kid by singing it in the barn and playing the tune on the big fiddle. The lumberjacks never could figure out whether Babe really enjoyed the song or whether Paul's singing gave him such a pain that he just couldn't help crying.

"I have a photograph of Paul's fiddle with Mr. Bridgewood standing beside it. The instrument is twelve feet long and four feet wide, and when the heel of the fiddle was tucked under Paul's chin he reached the keys easily with his left hand. The fiddle's neck was carved from a piece of ship timber ten feet long and fourteen inches wide, and the back and the front of the sounding box were glued with four-inch planks.

"Paul's fiddle is said to contain more than three hundred feet of selected Upper Peninsula lumber. When he played it the wind died down, Lake Superior became as calm as a mill pond, the tall Norways leaned over to listen, and the dickey birds swooned and fell from the trees, the music was so sweet and shivery. Sniffy McGurk said Paul's fiddling was regular cabalistic bewitchery. Ask any old northwoodsman who is proud of his fiddle and his playing, and he will tell you that never again will there be such heavenly music as Paul used to treat the boys to in the old white pine days.

"So, you see, Paul could turn his hand to almost anything and make a success of it. Even when times were dull he liked to keep busy. I remember that once upon a time when there were no logging contracts in sight, Paul contracted to deliver ten thousand post holes to some Escanaba people who were building an ore dock.

"When Paul signed this contract he had in mind a hole drilled years before in a search for oil near the Pickford fair ground. He drove Babe over to Pickford and made fast to the hole. Babe's very first tug pulled more than a thousand feet of it out of the ground, but when he kept on pulling the hole broke off. Paul worked for several days with Babe, trying to pull the balance of the hole out of the ground for shipment to Escanaba.

"Ever since that time there has been a flow of grand drinking water from what is left of the hole. Pickford folks are always glad to point out Paul Bunyan's flowing well to visitors. Paul's fiddle and the Pickford artesian well are mighty convincing answers to people that I call agnosticusses—the ones who have to be shown that Paul Bunyan actually lived here, logged off this great Upper Peninsula of ours and had a good time while doing it, to say nothing of many wonderful adventures.

"Everyone will agree that ample evidence of Paul Bunyan's life and heroic deeds among us has been presented in the foregoing. However, mention should be made of Paul's beehives, which stand today in various parts of upper Michigan just where he left them years ago.

"Paul built the beehives about the time we logged off the white pine limits in Marquette county. We ran the Laughing Whitefish River drive the same spring. The Laughing Whitefish is a crooked stream with plenty of sand bars, and many log jams had to be broken. Day after day Paul waded up to his waist in the cold water of the river, and before the drive was over he had a severe attack of rheumatism. The pain was sharp and his recovery was very slow. One day Peter White advised Paul to try the stings of bees.

"Now Paul had the same advice from several others, and he thought the experiment might be worth trying. He imported several thousand bees from a land to the southward—Madagascar, or Patagonia, or Texas, I think it was. When the bees arrived he turned them loose in his room, stripped and let them sting him from head to foot. The remedy was a strenuous one, but it worked. In a few days the rheumatism disappeared.

"Paul was grateful, and he called the bees his redhot little friends. He took swarms of the imported bees from camp to camp in the Upper Peninsula, and he built rows of giant beehives for them in places where sweet clover was abundant. The hives are constructed of stone and plaster and are well preserved. Summer tourists and visitors enjoy seeing and snap-shooting them.

"These stone hives are cone-shaped in the fashion of an ordinary beehive, but they are much larger. Some are fifteen feet high or more, and around them may still be seen the fields of hardy, enduring clover. Paul was fond of clover honey. He ate five pounds of honey every weekday and fifteen pounds with his Sunday dinners. He founded a bee research and experiment sta-

tion at Chatham, where bees were produced weighting more than
two pounds apiece. A lightning stroke was a gentle pat on the
back in comparison with one of Paul's bee stings.

"I mention Paul's imported bees because I am sure that everybody likes a good wildlife story," said Tim. "Paul built his beehives of stone, strong and lasting, at spots where they can be
found without trouble. A row of them stands beside highway
M-28 near Marquette and the shore of Lake Superior. However, it is not in very good condition, for Paul Bunyan fans have
taken many souvenir stone pieces from the hives. Another row
may be seen on the shore of Deer Lake near Onota. Many more
are still standing near Stephenson, in Menominee County.

"They are numerous, too, along the Portage Lake canal in
Houghton County, and dozens of them can be seen in Delta,
Schoolcraft and Luce counties, where Paul carried on heavy
woods operations and raised millions of bees. Paul planted acres
of clover for his imported bees at many places in the peninsula,
and they increased and multiplied and gave down tons of honey
until the winter of the blue snow, when swarms of them died and
the rest mysteriously disappeared.

"Years later, the first iron producers began to make charcoal
in the empty beehives, and they used the charcoal for fuel in their
furnaces. The hives were so well built that they suffered little
damage, and they remain to this day as visible proofs of Paul
Bunyan's operations in this territory.

"Some day Paul's remaining lumberjacks—only a few of us
are left—will place a bronze tablet, cast from Upper Peninsula
native copper, on each of Paul's beehives, or at least on one in
each row. These tablets will be about six feet square, and on
them there will be an inscription something like this:"

THIS BIG STONE BEEHIVE
Was Built By
The Great And Only
PAUL BUNYAN
For His Herds Of
Special Immigrant Bees
Imported From Madagascar
Or Somewhere Down South

———

MISTER BUNYAN
Was The
WORLD'S GREATEST LUMBERMAN-LOGGER
He Logged Off The
Upper Peninsula Of Michigan
In The '60s, The '70s,
And The '80s,
And He Liked His Clover Honey
Three Times A Day

———

Tablet Given By The Paul Bunyan
Lumberjacks' Protective Association
In Memory Of A Great Man

"But all I have told you about the relics of Paul Bunyan in the Upper Peninsula is nothing, compared to what you can see in the Paul Bunyan Museum at Blaney Park," concluded Truthful Tim.

"There the precious belongings of our greatest citizen are proof to the world that we treasure his memory and delight to honor Paul Bunyan, the outstanding logger of all time."

10

Alexander and Napoleon

While Paul Bunyan was recovering from his famous gallstone operation a long-debated question was settled at his Headquarters Camp—nothing less than the north country tomcat championship.

Over at Camp Twenty-Seven, Forty Jones had a cat—Napoleon by name—that was said to have licked a full-grown wolverine in a fair fight. The wolverine, everyone knew, was the toughest scrapper in the northwoods.

Napoleon policed the camp area in a gentlemanly way. He picked up a rabbit now and then and never looked for trouble. Once he brought in a couple of wolf cubs and laid them at Forty's feet. Forty wondered what had become of their mother. Napoleon, saying nothing, just looked wise and spat out gray hairs at intervals.

Every lumberjack knows that if you turn a house-cat loose in the woods it surely will take on weight. Raised in Manistique, Napoleon was just an ordinary cat until Forty took him out to camp. In six months he weighed thirty pounds and was a holy terror to stray dogs.

Johnny Inkslinger had a champion tomcat, too—Alexander the Great, the boys called him—at the Headquarters Camp. Aleck was a misfit gray monstrosity of a cat who bossed his particular area and no fooling. No woods rat ever ventured within a mile of the camp office. Only Elmer, the Moose Terrier, refused to take anything from Alexander, and Elmer was a truly mountainous dog.

Alexander knew that he was good. Paul Bunyan, Johnny Inkslinger and Truthful Tim could stroke his fur and welcome. Others hastened to sidestep that glaring eye and arched spine which humped itself when strangers or the common run of lumberjacks ventured near.

In Johnny's absence, Tim made up the payroll on a Saturday

for Camp Twenty-Seven, and took the money over to the lumberjacks housed there.

"You boys still game over at Headquarters?" asked Forty Jones when Tim was leaving. "Or do you think your moth-eaten cat has got a show? We're coming over to headquarters tomorrow, all hands and Napoleon. Maybe you've heard of Napoleon?"

"Yes, I've seen him. He's no match for Alexander."

"Is that so? We'll be there with bells on and lard in our hair, and oh, boy, what Napoleon won't do to that scarecrow of Johnny's. This camp has the best scrapper in the State of Michigan, bar none. Your gang's been doing some tall talking, but tell them we'll be there tomorrow afternoon with Napoleon and the long green."

That was enough for the Headquarters crew. They had money, too, and they fed Alexander on raw meat Saturday night and pulled his tail, to make him more cantankerous than usual. Yes, Alexander was in fighting trim, trained to the minute and stepping high, wide and handsome.

So the Headquarters crowd backed Alexander to the limit when the Camp Twenty-Seven crew arrived at 2 o'clock with Napoleon, who had objected strenuously to leaving home and was wondering what it was all about. He soon found out.

Before the argument opened Tim booked bets to the amount of all the ready money in both camps, plus dozens of IOUs. Each camp was sure that it just couldn't lose. They gathered in the big sleeping camp building, and all hands ranged themselves around the walls or sat on the bunks, and admired Alexander. He was purring around in a peaceful frame of mind when the door opened and Forty Jones gently pushed Napoleon into the arena.

Naturally Alexander resented this intrusion, just as you would if you were a tomcat in your own bailiwick and the master of all you surveyed, up to that fateful moment. He squared off in a most truculent manner, and at first Napoleon hesitated. Not that he was afraid, for Napoleon knew no fear. But when Alexander pfft-pffted in his face and bounded a hot left off Napoleon's bean, all that was generous in the latter vanished. The rich blood of his fighting Holkumnhmu ancestors surged through his veins and boiled over.

Instantly sensing that his antagonist would be a tough customer in a plain slugging match, Napoleon adopted the cautious, fancy style, based largely on speed, quick thinking and guerilla tactics, that made him the most famous cat in northern Michigan. His very first move had Alexander guessing and at a disadvantage from which he found it hard to recover and regain his poise.

Napoleon leaped high in the air, executed a barrel roll, and as he came down he grabbed a big pawful of fur off Alexander's only patch of white space. Alexander had always been mighty proud of his white section, and he couldn't let this unexpected action go by without a vigorous protest. He countered with a slashing hook that nicked Napoleon's ear and convinced the latter that this lad Alexander wasn't going to be put away without a struggle.

Now Napoleon, like his namesake, was one of the foxiest fighters that ever lived. He feigned distress and sat down, dizzy-like, with his ears drooping and his eyes half closed. This suckered Alexander into leading with another hook, but Napoleon went right in under it and tickled Aleck's chin with a scratch that brought the crimson.

Aleck figured that Napoleon had given him everything he had to offer, but he was underestimating the Holkumnhmu's analytical ability. He let go a sweeping five-clawed left that whistled like a dive-bomber, but Napoleon was in and out like a flash, and it merely grazed his whiskers.

Napoleon could see that it was his turn all right, so while Alexander was off balance he ripped a fast one along his opponent's ribs that sounded like a marimba tuning up. Then he high-stepped around, Gene Tunney style, and shook the fur from between his toes with Alexander stalking him.

Pretty soon Napoleon went up in the air again and did a perfect Immelmann turn high above Alexander. This confused Aleck and gave Napoleon a chance to step on his tail when descending. It enraged Alexander to a point where he got reckless and moved closer for a fine display of infighting. He rushed Napoleon and nearly bowled him over, but Poly ducked aside and as Aleck went by he played a xylophone solo on the gray cat's off ribs in a masterful display of generalship.

Alexander could see that he wasn't getting anywhere, so he sparred for time. He made a detour around the stove, figuring that he could take Napoleon by surprise in the rear. And at that he almost got the Camp Twenty-Seven champ, taking an impressive mittful of fur from behind Napoleon's sore ear. But this clever maneuver cost Alexander dearly, for Napoleon rolled over on his back and gave Aleck a kangaroo kick that had barbs in it, and how. It knocked Aleck clean across the sleeping camp and out of wind, while the lumberjacks gasped at the superhuman technique of the challenger. Even then Alexander couldn't see that he was fighting a master of the art, and he horned in for more.

By this time Napoleon had his man sized up, and he concluded that he could pick the final round and the style of scrapping. So he let Alexander come in close, figuring that a little rough stuff was overdue. He tagged Aleck's jowls with some nifty rights and lefts, and took a scratch over the eye himself.

They played pat-a-cake a bit, and Alexander speared Napoleon with a rear right well below the belt. It wasn't exactly according to Marquis of Queensberry rules, but Poly's protest didn't count, with no holds barred. Then Napoleon slapped Alexander's face with his tail and bit a chunk out of the back of his neck, while Alexander blinked and used some terrible language.

By this time Alexander was getting mean, and his true nature was beginning to show itself. He feinted with a right and raked Napoleon with a redhot left that opened a seam along Napoleon's shoulder blade.

Poly didn't like it, and he decided to quit fooling and to unloose his piece de resistance, which always does the business, and get it over with. He turned himself into a ball, rolled over and over till he had Aleck dizzy and groggy and wondering what it was all about, and then he suddenly exploded full in Aleck's face.

That ball was as full of claws and teeth as a porcupine with a thousand quills, and every one of them played a tattoo on Aleck's carcass. When Napoleon finally let up there was so much fur on the sleeping camp floor that it looked like somebody had busted grandma's feather tick and kicked it around.

Alexander dived under the big Quebec stove, and Forty Jones gathered up Napoleon lovingly, along with every last dime in the camp. As Poly went by the stricken Alexander in Forty's arms, he made a last triumphant pass at the fallen Headquarters' champ. Plainly he felt reasonably sure that the next time he visited Headquarters, Alexander would know who's boss and what's what. As for Aleck's supporters, they began to write home for money enough to keep them in snoos until the next pay day.

Along about six o'clock, Forty Jones and his gang, having surrounded all available refreshments at Headquarters Camp, left for home with the conquering Napoleon and all the money in that part of the world. The ones they left behind, with pockets turned inside out, could hear Forty and his men singing as they marched away in the twilight, the song that Lake Superior lumberjacks have sung for generations,

THE OLD GEEZERS

There was an old geezer
    Who had a wooden leg;
And it always was tobacco,
    For tobacco he would beg.

Another old geezer
    Who was cunning as a fox,
Always had tobacco
    In his old tobacco box.

Said the first old geezer,
    "Will you give to me a chew?"
Said the other old geezer,
    "I'll be hanged if I do.

"If you'd save all your pennies,
    Your dimes and your rocks,
Then you'd always have tobacco
    In your old tobacco box."

11

How Tall Was Paul?

Truthful Tim was reminiscing about Paul Bunyan's height. A thousand arguments have raged over that disputed point. Families have divided, communities sundered, and the Upper Peninsula almost brought to the point of secession from Michigan over the burning question—how tall was Paul?

"I don't recall that Paul Bunyan's height was ever measured by anyone in the camps where I worked," said Tim. "His woods clothing and his Sunday suits were made by a Cleveland tailor. Paul was sensitive about his size and he warned the tailor not to give out any information about his waist measure or other dimensions.

"However, I do remember certain particulars," Tim continued. "After I served a year as cookee Paul promoted me to a stool in the camp office, where I helped Johnny Inkslinger with the books and the payrolls. Later I was transferred to the van, or wanigan.

"What is a van? That's a natural question. You didn't spend your life in the pine woods, and you couldn't be expected to have the advantages that we lumberjacks enjoyed. So I hope you won't feel too downhearted if you find yourself not posted as well as the average lumberjack is.

"A van is the camp store maintained by every owner or manager of logging operations at his camp in the woods. Usually, but not always, the van was near the camp office and in the same log building. It offered goods wanted by the lumberjacks, such as woolen pants, jumpers, socks, coats, cotton work shirts, rubbers, high-cut boots, caps, candy, and eating and smoking tobacco.

"Most lumberjacks chew or smoke Peerless tobacco, while a few prefer fine cut. However, fine cut isn't considered good usage in the most approved lumberjack circles. We also sold snoos, which is the lumberjack's name for snuff. An occasional pinch of snuff clears the brain, peps up the mental faculties, and is a great help to the lumberjack who must do some hard thinking.

"At Paul's orders I took charge of the van and sold goods to the camp employees, usually on a time basis. The boys had little or no móney from Mondays to Saturdays and they generallv asked me to 'put the shot on the slate until pay day.' I filed a daily record of sales and cash receipts with Johnny Inkslinger. In the evenings, when I wasn't pursuing my studies for the ministry, I cobbled boots for the lumberjacks.

"One day Paul sent four cookees over to the van with one of his boots that was badly in need of a half sole. I spliced all the regular sized half soles in stock, one hundred or more, to make a half sole for Paul's big boot. The job required nineteen spools of waxed thread measuring six hundred yards to the spool.

"I took my time and did a first class repair job for Paul, and and he was so pleased that he sent the other boot to the van to be half soled too. But my supply of sole leather was exhausted. I was up a tree and out on a limb for a minute, and then I had a grand idea.

"We received a carload of pancake flour weekly, and a couple of thousand pounds of it were required for each morning's flapjacks. I sent five hundred extra pounds of flour over to the cook camp, and asked Sourdough Sam to make up for me a special batch of his very best flapjacks. When they were delivered at the van, smoking hot from the griddle, I spliced them together carefully, half soled the second boot with them and returned it to Paul. Months later he told me that the flapjack sole was outwearing the leather one by a big margin. This incident shows clearly that Paul was a big man, also that Sourdough Sam made dependable flapjacks.

"Paul was taller than Big Ole, the camp blacksmith. When Paul took a chew of Peerless tobacco he stowed away five packages of the weed one by one. When the last package was safely packed in his cheek a bright and cheerful look came over his face. But people who didn't know that Paul's south cheek was stuffed with eating tobacco were sure the poor man was suffering from toothache.

"The boys enjoyed seeing Paul eat his tobacco and shift his cud. They said that when the time came for him to spit, some of the more timid ones began to shed their clothes and prepared to take the swells. But that was just their little joke.

"An Iron River writer has said that Paul was only ten feet in height. The evidence presented was the number of Peerless packages eaten by Paul at one sitting. But Sniffy McGurk ate eight packages of Peerless and four rolls of fine cut one morning, and Sniffy isn't a large man.

"Paul looked high and proud, like an eagle. He was a grand sight, with his big blue eyes blazing under bushy eyebrows, and a moustache like a flock of bicycle handle bars. In cold weather he sported a black beard wide and deep enough to house a hundred chimney swallows. With the coming of spring his whiskers turned a delicate shade of green, and he shaved them clean without delay, but the moustache was a permanent ornament. The boys said that when Paul's alfalfa took on an emerald hue it was time to go fishing, and sure enough, the ice always went out in the spring within twenty-four hours of the first changing tint in his whiskers.

"But let's get back to the van. The neck band of Paul's shirts measured thirty-nine inches. He sat down while I climbed a twelve-foot ladder to take his neck size. This demonstrates that he was a very tall man, and big all over. When he dressed up he wore an Oddfellow pin that measured three feet each way. It must have weighed forty pounds, but it nestled like a rose in the lapel of Paul's coat.

"I have heard that it took seventy yards of blue corduroy cloth to make a pair of Sunday pants for Paul, and six quarter-mile spools of thread. I can well believe that, for I measured his boot laces while I was making the half soles for them. They were twenty-six feet long and very strong and tough.

"One winter we logged the pine around Sardine Can lake in Baraga county. Babe broke his harness tugs while hauling a load of logs up the hills. Paul was in a hurry, and his brain worked like lightning when he resolved to turn his boot laces into tugs. He lashed them to the sleighs and hitched them on to Babe's yoke. Babe hauled thirty-eight loads of logs up L'Anse hill, which everybody knows is one of the longest and steepest in the country, using Paul's boot laces for harness tugs. We simply must agree that Paul was a giant of a man.

"Paul's bed sheets were more than twenty-five feet long. They had to be long in order to cover him. One night I heard him snoring so loudly that the dishes rattled in the cook camp. I peeked into his bunk room and saw that his shoulders and arms were uncovered while his feet were sticking over the foot of the bed. You can see from this that Paul was an unusually large man.

"He told me once that the premiums on his life insurance policies cost six times the rate for a man of ordinary size. We might imply from this that he was six times as tall as the average man. Maybe the companies charged Paul an extra rate because he led an adventurous life. They knew he spent most of his time in the woods, and maybe they feared a tree would fall on him or that the wolves and the bears might eat him before his time.

"Not long after Paul went away, my pal Sniffy McGurk and I were arguing the old question in the back of the van one day— how tall was Paul? One-Eye LaRue, the barn boss, had sent over some special brew moonshine that was full of authority. It had snapped the hoops off the keg in which he stored it, and cracked several bottles. He sent over what was left of it in a heavy stone jug, and every now and then the jug sizzled.

"Sniffy had a couple of snorts. He took a big pinch of snuff and I could see that he was thinking hard. 'Now let's be conservative about this,' he said, 'and figure it out on a reasonable basis. We know it never took less than eighty cookees to grease the big griddle that fried the flapjacks for Paul's breakfast. Allowing sixty cookees for the center of the griddle, that leaves twenty to grease the edges, doesn't it?' He took another drink, totted up mentally and continued:

" 'Now, I should say that each cookee was a little over five feet tall. Laying your cookees end to end, you get one hundred and ten feet of cookees. Dividing the result by three point one four one six, as we were told to do by the professors at Michigan Tech who have been working on the same problem, we find the diameter of Paul's griddle to be approximately thirty-five feet and something over. Let's have a drink.' He took another pinch of snuff and was in deep thought for a while.

" 'So far, so good,' he said after mentally checking the result. 'To proceed. Seeing that the diameter of an ordinary flapjack griddle is say a foot and a quarter, we ascertain from this that Paul's griddle was about twenty-eight times bigger than ordinary. I hope that's plain to you, because I've put in hours and hours figuring it out.

" 'Therefore,' says Sniffy—he was clever with figures and he liked to work in a dollar and a quarter word now and then—'we can consistently infer from this that Paul Bunyan was twenty-eight times as tall as the average man. That makes his height approximately one hundred and fifty-four feet. Get me, and do you perceive any miscomputation in my argument pro and con?'

"Well, I didn't talk back to Sniffy. He could add and subtract and use language better than I could, anyway. I never was much good at figures. If the jug hadn't cracked and spilled the rest of the moonshine, Paul would have been twenty times as tall as Goliath ever was."

12

Paul Harnesses Lake Superior

"No one ever dreamed of putting Lake Superior, the world's largest freshwater body, to work for mankind until Paul Bunyan saw the chances. He is the man who tamed Lake Superior after everyone else was convinced that it could not be mastered," continued Tim.

"There must have been an affinity—if you know what I mean —between Paul and Lake Superior. In the end the biggest lake fairly ate out of the hand of the world's biggest man. It took more than a wide sheet of water to bluff Paul Bunyan. But I think he loved Lake Superior and I know that he never strayed far from its shores.

"On one occasion he contracted with Jim Hill to fence the Great Northern railway lines from St. Paul and Minneapolis to Seattle. His bid was away below all the others, and his competitors predicted that Paul would go broke that year for certain. But he fooled them. He assembled five hundred trained Upper Peninsula beavers and two thousand gophers, and placed them in camps properly spaced all the way between Duluth, St. Paul and the Coast. The beavers cut the posts and the gophers dug the holes; and although Paul took the contract at very low figures, he made a satisfactory profit on the deal. That was the farthest away from Lake Superior that he ever traveled."

As a small boy plays with a puddle, so did Paul play with Lake Superior. The first dam he built across St. Mary's rapids at Sault Ste. Marie raised the Lake Superior water level twenty feet, and thus he provided ample depths for his log booms and harbors along the south shore, according to Tim.

Walking around the lake one day, Paul conceived a plan for making a new freshwater fishing record. Pete Vigeant had been catching some whoppers in St. Mary's River, and Paul resolved to beat Pete's highest mark.

Paul dynamited a hill beyond the north shore of Lake Superior in the Height of Land country, and this started the Nipigon River flowing northward into Hudson's Bay. Following up his scheme to monopolize the best freshwater fishing in the world, he opened a hole in the dam at Sault Ste. Marie, checked the river's southward flow, and soon the big fish in the lower lakes were following the reversed current up St. Mary's river into Lake Superior.

For a time Paul's efforts were richly rewarded. He caught muskellunge weighing more than one hundred pounds, Mackinaw trout weighing two hundred pounds, and sturgeon five hundred pounds. Pete Vigeant, Fred Stephenson, Dr. Christofferson and other famous fishermen threatened to have the law on Paul.

Within a month, however, the Lake Superior level went down thirty feet and St. Mary's rapids went nearly dry, but Paul made a world's fishing record. In order to restore normal water levels, Paul blew up a range of mountains on the north shore, bringing the Nipigon's flow into Lake Superior as before. The blast shook the Upper Peninsula and rocked the country as far away as Bananas, Texas. The ground weaved and heaved like Lake Superior in a storm, and various copper, iron and gold formations were brought to the surface in many places. The tremendous shock of the explosion made the great Lake Superior mining industry possible. The mine owners and miners are grateful to Paul's memory, for it was he who made mining not only possible but profitable over a wide area.

The winter of '86 was very cold, and at the end of December the lake was frozen to the bottom. Paul was logging at Pieface lake near Munising bay when he held his annual New Year party, the big social event of the year in the north country.

A friend had sent Paul a cask of kummel, and it was tapped while the party was under way. On New Year's day at two o'clock in the afternoon, Paul was feeling sprightly and cheerful, and he allowed that the time had come to show Lake Superior who was boss.

He placed the yoke on Babe and drove the big ox to the lake shore. Then he hitched Babe to a corner of the frozen lake, drank six dishpans full of black coffee, swallowed a pitcher of kummel

and another of aquavit, gave Babe a lusty kick, and yelled
"GIDDAP!"

Smoothly, irresistibly, in less than five minutes Babe hauled
that enormous mass of ice out of its basin and up to the shore
south of Munising and the Pictured Rocks. Paul surveyed it
calmly and stroked his whiskers as he drank the rest of the
kummel. Then he grabbed a log measuring six feet in diameter
and hundreds of feet in length, and peavied the great berg into
the place he had picked for it. From that position when spring
came, the melting ice would drip into the basin and become Lake
Superior once more. That was just like Paul—always doing something spectacular. A man who could boss Lake Superior around
like that couldn't help being famous.

The big lake was Paul's ice-house for many years. When he
began logging on a large scale he built half a dozen ice-houses at
points around the south shore of the lake all the way from Sault
Ste. Marie to Duluth. This plan of storing ice, however, was not
very satisfactory. The cookees would sneak into the buildings
and smoke cigarettes there, and Paul lost one or more ice-houses
by fire each year.

When Paul kept a dozen camps going at once, all of the ice
from Lake Superior was needed to supply his summer camps. The
men began to cut ice in January near Fort William and Port
Arthur, and they sawed cakes weighing five hundred pounds
each all the way across the lake to the south shore. It was a
huge task to haul out the ice and store it in the houses.

Johnny Inkslinger, always planning to reduce operating costs,
conceived the idea of making Lake Superior its own ice-house.
Paul adopted the plan, and in the following winter the crews
cut the usual forty million cakes, but they didn't store the ice
on land. They weighted the cakes as soon as they were cut and
sank them to the bottom of the lake, tying buoys to each cake
and thus marking its location.

Paul's camps were never very far from Lake Superior, and the
cakes were hoisted as needed in summer. The lake bottom was
cool and the loss by melting was much less than it would have
been on shore. This plan of storing ice was followed for years
and it worked perfectly. The crews cut ice as usual in the last

winter that Paul Bunyan spent on the Earth, and the cakes were anchored to the bottom of the mighty lake.

Then Paul went away, and not very long afterward the camps broke up. Millions of ice cakes remained in the lake, and this is the secret of Lake Superior's intensely cold water, as explained by an Englishman who visited the Upper Peninsula a few years ago. Speaking to a reporter about some of the extraordinary things he had seen and heard while in the States, he said:

"You know, the water in Lake Superior is frightfully cold. It's most singular, too, that the water should be so much colder than the water in any other of the Great Lakes.

"It was indeed interesting to me to learn of the curious American custom that causes this coolness," he went on. "I was informed by a gentleman in Calumet that each winter the ice freezes to a depth of twenty or thirty feet—just fancy!

"The harvesting of the ice crop, he assures me, is the chief industry of the laboring classes. The ice is cut into enormous blocks, so large that it would be difficult to lift them. These blocks are weighted down with shot and attached with ropes to buoys, and sunk to the bottom of the lake. A most ingenious idea, is it not?

"When the big cakes are needed they are floated to the surface, towed to the shore and cut up. The whole bottom of the lake is paved with ice blocks, I am told. The custom was instituted many years ago by a large person named Paul Bunyan, I understand. He had several logging camps not far from the lake.

"It's a most extraordinary thing, but one can't help seeing that this is why the water is so cold, can't one? It's really a lake of ice water, you know. So I am telling them at home that the Americans are so fond of iced water that they keep a whole lake of it in the States. Curious idea, isn't it? But so cleverly American, don't you know!"

There isn't a doubt that the greater part of Paul's final ice harvest has never melted and is still lying on the floor of the lake. So now you know just why Lake Superior water is so cold.

At one time or another, it is estimated, Paul Bunyan owned more than one-half of the Upper Peninsula woodlands. He opened his first saw mill in the spring of '81. In it and in others built later he turned millions of his own and other owners' logs into lumber, lath and shingles. He decided to carry his timber products to market in his own freighter, and he built and launched the largest ship that ever sailed on Lake Superior. Its capacity was equal to that of ten ordinary lumber carriers, or "hookers," as they are called in the Lake Superior country.

A committee of lumberjacks suggested that the ship be christened the PAUL BUNYAN. It was so big that Paul mounted the captain and the mates on horses taken from Paul's lumber camps, so they could hustle around the decks in a hurry and give orders to the crew.

The masts of the PAUL BUNYAN were so tall that the officers had to use telescopes when looking aloft at the sailors in the crow's nest, and they didn't shout orders to the sailors up there, they telephoned them. The topmasts were hinged and they could be lowered to let the clouds go by, but the masts didn't have to be lowered when the moon passed, as some folks have stated who were careless with the truth. The masts were tall, to be sure, but they weren't as tall as that.

The PAUL BUNYAN sailed Lake Superior for years. When it came into port business ceased uptown and the entire community hastened to the dock for a better sight of the monster. After the first year none but boy sailors were shipped on the PAUL BUNYAN. It was found that mature men who were sent aloft seldom returned to the deck before developing long gray beards. Yes, the PAUL BUNYAN was a big ship,—too big, some people thought.

When his giant lumber hooker went into commission on Lake Superior, Paul contracted with a dredging concern for the tearing out of a section of his dam across the river at Sault Ste. Marie. Then he built the first ship canal and lock for the use of the PAUL BUNYAN in delivering his timber products to Detroit and Chicago, Cleveland, Milwaukee and Buffalo. But Johnny Inkslinger, who had drawn the plans, specified a draft of only twenty-one feet of water over the lock mitre sills, and the PAUL BUNYAN drew twenty feet of water light and forty feet loaded.

It looked like a serious mistake, and the managers of rival boat lines swore that Paul was nothing but a checkmated amateur as a lumber carrier. But Paul fooled 'em. He built another ship below the locks, named the TINY, and put her on a time schedule with the PAUL BUNYAN. The big boat on Lake Superior sailed down to the rapids with one hundred million feet of lumber aboard. The crew unrolled an endless chain machine which extended down through the rapids, and conveyed the lumber from the PAUL BUNYAN, anchored above, to the TINY, anchored below, at the rate of one million feet a minute. The entire cargo was transferred in not more than an hour and ninety minutes.

"Lake Superior had its revenge in the fall of '86, I think it was, when a storm wrecked the PAUL BUNYAN on a reef off the coast of Isle Royale. The ship sank keel down in two hundred fathoms of water alongside the reef. I understand the Government makes use today of the mainmast as a lighthouse. The light is hundreds of feet above water level and it can be plainly seen fifty miles away. After Paul left us, the good ship TINY was converted into a municipal pier at Chicago. Not many people of the thousands who use the pier daily know that it was once the property of the famous logger Paul Bunyan," said Tim.

When Paul found that the lock and ship canal at Sault Ste. Marie would be of no particular use to him because of their shallow depth, he presented them to Uncle Sam's Government, which is making use of them in transporting considerable quantities of iron ore, wheat and coal around the rapids. He sold the stone power house and other buildings he had erected below the rapids, and great quantities of calcium carbide are made there now.

More ship locks were built by U.S. engineers, and Paul's dam above the rapids was raised and strengthened. This caused Lake Superior to flood its shore lines for miles. The spring overflow thawed thousands of giant bullfrogs that had been buried in the mud of the great Tahquamenon swamp. More than once the bullfrogs raided Paul's camps in the night and stole many of Sourdough Sam's chickens.

All this happened about the time that Paul changed the location of Grand Island, which formerly lay out in Lake Superior fifty miles north of Munising and the Pictured Rocks. Paul ordered the captain of the PAUL BUNYAN to tow the island to the mouth of Munising Bay, where the pines on it could be logged with less trouble.

One of the bullfrogs croaked hoarsely in the night as the PAUL BUNYAN brought the island in. The captain was sure he heard the Grand Marais fog horn in the dark and he kept too far to starboard. That was the night that the PAUL BUNYAN rammed the shore and made the big dent that you see in the hills where the city of Munising stands today.

Paul tamed one of the big bullfrogs and made a pet of it. The frog hung around the cook camp most of the time and begged for Sourdough Sam's sinkers. When Sam held out a sinker the frog sat up on its hind legs and barked—or croaked—until the sinker was dropped into its wide-open mouth.

One day Peter White, Paul's boyhood friend, came down from Marquette to the camp. Paul said to him: "Peter, I have a bullfrog that weighs forty-eight pounds." Peter said: "Paul, I have five dollars that say you don't know what you're talking about. There never was any such animal."

So they put up five dollars apiece with Johnny Inkslinger and the frog was weighed on the store scales. It weighed nineteen pounds. "Ah, ha," said Peter, "the money is mine." "Wait a minute, Peter," said Paul, "this bullfrog is different. He's nineteen pounds frog and twenty-nine pounds bull." So Paul won the bet, and he bought Peter a good five-cent cigar.

Paul wrote some verses about his pet bullfrog that were printed in a Detroit paper. Many other poets were jealous when Paul's verses won a poetry contest in the Police Gazette. Here is one of the stanzas:

> What a wonderful bird the frog are!
>   When he stands up, he sits down—almost;
> When he hops, he flies—almost;
>   He ain't got no tail hardly, either.
> When he sits down, he sits on what he ain't got—almost;
>   What a wonderful, wonderful bird the frog are!

13

The Paul Bunyan Echo

The Paul Bunyan echo is a remarkable phenomenon. Scientists come to the Pictured Rocks from all over the world to investigate it, and it never has been satisfactorily explained.

Along with Paul's beautiful colored drawings on the high sandstone bluffs it has made the Pictured Rocks famous through the Earth. The Pictured Rocks, twenty-two miles long and a couple of hundred feet high, extend along the south shore of Lake Superior in Alger County, from a point near Munising to Beaver Lake, not far from the Nagow Wudjoo sand dunes and Grand Marais.

Longfellow and Paul Bunyan are back of the great popularity of the Pictured Rocks and the sand dunes. You no doubt recollect that Pau-Puk-Keewis danced his Beggar's Dance on the sand dunes, as related in Longfellow's immortal poem. Later he had a fight with Hiawatha and ran to shelter in a Pictured Rocks cave which was struck by Waywassimo, the lightning, crushing Pau-Puk-Keewis to death when the roof fell in.

Of course that was long before Paul Bunyan sailed along the foot of the rocks and painted and carved them with startling designs on summer afternoons. Some of his lumberjacks are of the opinion that Paul installed the echo secretly while he was doing the painting and carving which attract so many visitors. He liked nothing better than to sail on the big lake with Tiny in his skiff, which was an eighth of a mile long. They floated close to the rocky bluffs for hours, fishing and halting now and then while Paul drew and cut his fantastic designs on the living rock.

He liked to talk with the echo. He would maneuver his skiff to a certain point on the lake southwest of Miner's Castle, exactly one hundred and seventeen feet from shore. Then he stood up and called loudly: "PAUL!"

In four and a half seconds, back came the voice of the echo: "PAUL! WHICH PAUL? WHY, PAUL BUNYAN, OF COURSE!"

You see, it is the nature of the reply that makes the Paul Bunyan echo so unique. The echo talks back just like a human being. For instance, let us suppose that some other name than Paul's is mentioned by the caller. He stands up in his boat at the right spot from shore and shouts, for example: "JOHNSON!"

In four and a half seconds the echo replies in a wild and offended tone: "To HELL WITH JOHNSON, AND WHERE'S PAUL BUNYAN?"

This shows that the most astounding of all echoes is thinking of its creator, Paul Bunyan. It actually gets angry when some other name is used. The echo is one of the scientific mysteries of the age, and its still operates clearly, but the listener must be very careful to keep his boat at just the right distance from Miner's Castle.

Paul decorated the Pictured Rocks in the same year that he logged at the Sucker river, east of Beaver lake.

"I must tell you how he changed the course of the Sucker. It's a good story," continues Truthful Tim.

"Once the Sucker River flowed north into Lake Superior, but every lumberjack knows that Paul Bunyan made a new channel for it which directs the river's flow into Grand Marais creek and thence into Grand Marais harbor.

"Some folks who no doubt mean well have undertaken to change the name of Sucker River and Sucker Lake to Succor. The Paul Bunyan Lumberjacks' Protective Association is fighting this move, in the interests of truth and decency and historical values. In our opinion, it's a crime to think of changing the name of Sucker River, which was the scene of a most remarkable happening in Paul Bunyan's time.

"I never will forget the spring of '79, when we ran the Sucker River drive. We cut in the previous winter, and watered that spring, seventy million feet of top quality white pine logs. The water was about as high as usual for that time of the year.

"We broke the jams at the bends in the shallows, drove the logs down and boomed them at the river mouth. We were all ready to shoot them into Lake Superior, where two of Paul's tugs stood by with more boomsticks. Once the raft was made up, the logs would be towed to the Big Bay saw mill.

"On a Sunday morning after breakfast Paul came into the sleeping camp and said: 'Boys, I want you to have a good rest today. There's a hard day ahead of us tomorrow, making up the raft.'

"Our camp was on the shore of the river about a mile from Lake Superior. Early Monday morning Paul walked over to the river and was astonished to find that every log had disappeared. The channel had been crowded with logs the night before. Paul rubbed his eyes and stared around, but not a log was to be seen. At first he thought that the boom at the river's mouth had broken and let the logs float out into the lake. But in a few minutes we knew that something mighty unusual had occurred. We saw Paul hopping around like a madman on the river bank. He was waving his fists in the air and using bad language.

"We hurried over to the river, and what a sight was there! Millions of suckers, weaving, crowding, gleaming in the morning sunlight, all trying to swim up the river at once on their spring spawning run. They had formed a living, moving, resistless wall which had shoved our entire winter's cut of pine back up and out of the river. In some places the timber had been pushed clear over the river banks a quarter of a mile back in the woods. It was a heart-breaking spectacle. We could see that Paul was justified in using language, and we helped him use it.

"Paul had to bring in a dipper dredge to scoop the suckers out of the channel before we could roll the logs back into the river. The fish were piled twenty feet high in the woods, where they were left when the water went down. Sniffy McGurk figured that we hoisted not less than fourteen millions of shiny, slippery suckers and toted them out to deep water. He had the best head for figures I ever saw.

"Paul issued orders to the cooks and the cookees to salt down five hundred barrels of suckers. Sourdough Sam fed us fried, boiled and baked suckers, sucker pie, sucker fish balls and sucker salad three times a day. Since that time I haven't cared any more for suckers than I have for beans," added Tim.

"When the raft was safely started for Big Bay, Paul figured up the losses caused by the big run of suckers. He estimated them at not less than $25,000. At his orders we went to work with a will and changed the course of the river, and I am sure that such a calamity can never happen again."

Every lumberjack knows that the south shore of Lake Superior and the north shores of Lake Huron and Lake Michigan were the logical place for Paul Bunyan to live and carry on his logging work. There was good reason for calling Lake Superior Paul Bunyan's millpond. Didn't he conquer the big lake and raise or lower it at will? He floated his lumber carrier and his rafts and tugs on its water, dammed it at the St. Mary's river outlet, and built the big power house at Sault Ste. Marie which made Lake Superior work for him.

In his prime and when the weather was warm, Paul often drank four hundred gallons of water an hour. The fact is, he didn't dare to stray very far from Lake Superior in summer, or at least from a place where drinking water was plentiful. He never could have become a genius or a giant if he had lived on the dry western plains.

Paul took a drink of something else now and then, but he didn't let it interfere with business. Hanging on the wall of his office was a copy of a poem which he said was written by a man named Epick Cure Us, years and years ago. It read:

> If on my theme I rightly think,
>   There are five reasons why men drink;
> Good wine, a friend, because I'm dry,
>   Or lest I should be by and by,
>   Or any other reason why.

Paul said it was good poetry and good sound sense, but the lumberjacks never did really understand it. When they felt like taking a drink they took it, and didn't ask themselves why. Paul said that he took a drink only on two occasions—when he was alone, and when there was somebody with him. The boys enjoyed his little jokes. They showed that he was feeling bright and cheerful and probably was making money. As long as Paul joked every lumberjack felt reasonably sure of his job.

Paul always felt especially good after visiting his girl Tiny. She lived in Germfask. She was a blonde, all pink and white and gold, and her blue eyes were as fascinating as a snake's. When

Paul and Tiny walked down Main street together folks turned their heads for a second look at Tiny, so little and fair and fluffy, and at Paul, so big and dark and proud and happy looking.

Paul thought the world of Tiny, and she may have loved him, too. But she played false with him once, and he had a bad night when he came back to camp after finding out that she was attending a dance with another man. That time he took one drink too many. When he awoke next morning after sleeping off a heavy load, he wanted a drink powerful bad. He stepped to the door and hollered for whiskey. Barney McGinnis, sitting in his saloon five miles away at Grand Marais, came out of a doze with a start and shoved out a bottle on the bar. Paul surely had a pine-top voice.

One Sunday Paul drove down the old woods road to see Tiny. He had just bought a shining new buggy and the fastest horse in the north country. He was wearing a new suit and his moustache smelled of roses.

When he was crossing the Fox river bridge south of Seney his new straw hat blew into the river. The water was high and his pants were creased, so he stopped the horse, took off his clothes and put them in the buggy and swam out for the hat.

When he got back to the road the horse was headed for Germfask and nearly out of sight down the road. Paul stood on the bridge, all dressed up in a straw hat and with no place to go. I expect he used language as he started down the pike in the altogether after the horse. Luckily there was no one else on the highway at the time. Any traveler who might have happened along would have had the sensation of a lifetime.

Paul ran like the wind after his skittish horse, drew alongside the buggy and climbed in without stopping it. He proceeded to dress in a hurry. He had slipped his shirt on over his head and was reaching for his pants when Tiny suddenly turned the corner just ahead. She had walked up the road to meet Paul and she was delighted to see him.

Paul's first impulse was to keep going, but his hands involuntarily drew the reins and the horse stopped. Tiny placed her foot on a wheel hub and jumped into the buggy a fraction of a second after Paul grabbed the lap robe and whisked it over his bare legs.

"Oh Paul," said Tiny, "I'm so glad you're here at last, and what made you so late? Just give me some of that lap robe,—" and with that she pulled it toward her. With a gasp and a gurgle Paul hurdled over the buggy wheel and disappeared in the woods, trailing his pants behind him.

"Well, he came out pretty soon, red in the face but with his pants on," said Truthful Tim. "I guess Paul never did make Tiny understand just what he was doing in that buggy minus his pants. But then, a little thing like that couldn't disturb a real love affair, could it?

"For months Paul and Tiny looked like a match to us lumberjacks," continued Tim. "We tried to guess the day of their marriage. We spent whole evenings speculating on the future of such a marriage—mostly the physical part of it. You see, Tiny was so little, and Paul was so big—how could such a union ever be consummated? And suppose she came down with child. Could she ever mother Paul's baby?

" 'Tiny never can have a child by Paul Bunyan,' Johnny Inkslinger told me. 'You mark my words, it's impossible. There's no use thinking about it.'

"But Chris Crosshaul said Johnny was talking through his hat. 'What does Johnny know about women? I've had four wives, and I'm a husky cuss, but any one of 'em was too much for me. I'm telling you Tiny could mother a dozen of Paul's kids and then outlast him twenty years.'

"These interesting speculations were brought to a rude close when Tiny went to a dance with Con Kilhane. Con was cock of the walk in the Emerson country, a fine strapping timber jobber. His first question of the man applying for a job with him was— 'Kin ye fight?' If the newcomer gave a good account of himself in a friendly slugging match with the boss, he was given a job forthwith.

"Paul felt that Tiny had two-timed him with Con, and he lay in wait for the latter when Con visited Germfask. Kilhane wasn't as tall as Paul, but there was more hair on his chest than there was on Paul's, and every lumberjack knows that is the signmark of a good fighter," said Tim. "It was the battle of the century in the fair north country, and they're still talking about it.

"They met in Angus McDougall's bar, and the preliminaries were polite and snappy," continued Tim. "Con wasn't afraid of any man living, not even Paul Bunyan. Con knew that Paul was looking for trouble. He walked up to Paul with that devil-may-care Irish grin on his face, and yelled: 'Kin ye fight?' and followed up the defy with a smash on Paul's jaw that would have put an ordinary man through the side of the building. In the same split second Paul slapped Con clean over the bar into Angus's stock of Three-Star Hennessey and Angostura Bitters.

"But that didn't faze Con. He was used to knocking and being knocked around, and flying heels over head into a back bar couldn't stop him. Angus shooed them into the street—it wasn't much of a street then, half a dozen houses and Angus's store and bar, with the woods crowding in everywhere—and they gave each other a six-hour classic mauling that never will be forgotten in lumberjack circles.

"Soon Paul's chin was bleeding and Con was spitting big white teeth in two directions. Con was as hairy as a bear, but when Paul's ham-like fists scrunched into the pads on his breast and shoulders, great welts rose beneath the black and sweaty curls.

"When they clinched and weaved and strained, they knocked over virgin timber all the way from the river to the hill where cleared farms are now. It was a fair and square fight—no eye-gouging, no biting, no knee in the groin; they slugged each other hour after hour up and down the river bank while the awed inhabitants, including Tiny, looked on; and when they tired of that they stood knee to knee and fought.

"When darkness fell, Paul and Con were still battling with right good will—Paul with puffed lips, a battered chin, torn ear and liver-colored eye; Con minus a dozen teeth and sporting a bloody nose which spouted crimson over both fighters. Spectators said that Con might have had a trifle the best of the argument when he caught one of Paul's lefts under his ear, tripped over a root and landed on his head in the river, coming down on a rock that stunned him and left him half lifeless on the shallow bottom.

"Night was at hand, the darkness intensified by the brush and bracken torn up by those mighty heels and obscuring the sky. Paul jumped into the river—they had splashed half the water out of it—and fished Con out. They went up the road a piece and had a drink with Angus on the corner where the argument started. They clinked glasses and Con said, with all the admiration in the world: 'Ye sure kin fight.'

"That's the Lake Superior country for you," said Tim. "Have your argument out like men, and don't nurse any grudges afterward. The two were friends forever after."

"And what became of Tiny?" we asked.

"Didn't you know that Tiny married Con a couple of weeks after the fight?" said Tim. "She led him a dog's life; married him out of pity, I suppose. Paul Bunyan always was a lucky guy."

14

Elmer, the Moose Terrier

Elmer, the moose terrier, was the world's most remarkable dog. He was a large dog—more than twelve feet long and built in proportion. He lived on moose meat and liverwurst, and nothing else. Folks were sometimes critical when they saw Elmer loafing around a logging camp and eating half a barrel of Milwaukee braunschweiger at a meal. It did seem like a sinful waste of good sausage, but Elmer never failed to pay his way in the moose hunting season.

Elmer loved to hunt moose. When Paul hollered, "Moose, Elmer, moose!" Elmer would cock up one ear and then the other, and nod his head, as much as to say, "I get you, boss, old top," and then he would tear into the woods. Soon he would trot home carrying a full-grown moose over his shoulder. If Sourdough Sam was short of meat Elmer would keep right on hunting and bringing in moose until Sam reckoned that he had enough moose meat for the day.

It was as good as a play to see Elmer bring in a moose, toting it over his shoulder and holding an ear or a horn in his teeth. He knew who was boss, too. When he found Paul Bunyan, he would lay the carcass at Paul's feet, wag his tail, crouch down and shake hands with Paul, just as if he might be saying: "Well, boss, here's more meat for you and me and the boys, and thanks for the liverwurst. Then Paul would pat Elmer on the head and swell around and say: "Boys, d'ye see that dawg? I raised him from a pup!"

Elmer was the wisest dog that ever lived. He knew almost everything there was to know. When Paul took down his rifle, Elmer would race over and chase a moose out of the swamp. If Paul reached for his shotgun Elmer would rush around and flush a bird. If Sourdough Sam picked up a milk pail Elmer would round up Lucy, the camp cow, and back her into position for milking. When Elmer saw Paul take down his fish pole he would scoot behind the barn and dig a can of worms. He could even wash dishes without breaking them, that is, tin dishes. There never was a dog like Elmer. He was in a class of his own.

One cold February day a mad moose caught Elmer off guard up on Screw Auger creek, and attacked him. Paul saw the moose knock Elmer down and trample him, but Paul's gun wasn't loaded. All he had for ammunition was the powder from a broken shell.

Paul was a mighty quick thinker and he could see that Elmer was in great danger. He said afterward that the cold sweat fairly boiled out of him at the terrible sight. When the sweat beads fell from his forehead they froze solid and fell on the snow as hard as bullets.

That gave Paul a good idea. He slipped several of the frozen beads into the muzzle of his gun, on top of the powder. He ran towards the moose, who was stamping Elmer into the snow by this time, and fired. The sweat beads shot out of the gun, but the explosion melted them. As the drops hurtled through the air they froze solid again, this time in long, pointed icicles, and the icicles stabbed the moose to death just in time to save Elmer from destruction. Paul said it was the closest call that Elmer ever had.

Elmer was a dependable dog except when he met up with a moose in the woods. When that happened he forgot everything else. He toted the weenies to the woods crew on the hot dog sled on winter days and that, of course, made him famous. But faithful as he was, if he spied a moose when he went steaming down the road, it was too bad for the woods crew that morning.

In the end a moose was Elmer's downfall. No matter where a moose went Elmer couldn't resist the urge to chase it. One winter when Paul was logging at Betsey Lake, Elmer followed a moose out on the Lake Superior ice. The ice was only four feet thick that winter, and Elmer broke through and drowned. The moose kept going and got away to Canada.

15

Tige, Son of Elmer

It was on a fine spring morning in '77 that Paul Bunyan hiked down to Sault Ste. Marie from Rag Bag Lake, up Paradise way, where his small camp of a scant thousand lumberjacks was nearing the end of its winter's cut. The distance was sixty miles—just a mere after-breakfast stroll for Paul.

He had serious business in the Sault that day, but as he came over the hill and down the St. Ignace trail and Plank Alley to the river, he found the few business houses closed and deserted. He heard a steamer whistle, and making his way down Water Street past the old Johnston home, he found the entire population of the town on the pier and the good ship Michigan pulling in. It was the first boat of the season from Detroit.

The Michigan docked, and deck hands and dock men proceeded to unload freight. Soon five hundred barrels of beer and five barrels of flour were piled high on the pier.

Paul was amazed, dumbfounded. He walked around the pile, trying to figure it out. He took a big pinch of snoos, thought harder than ever, and finally gave it up. "I wonder what in the tarnation blazes they're going to do with all that flour," he mused.

Paul knew his Salteurs, and they knew him, and what he was there for. He was to plead that day before Justice of the Peace Mark W. Smith, the case of his friend Louis Poissin against Auguste Le Fave—the action being a suit for damages against La Fave for the killing of Poissin's dog.

The dog had been Paul's gift to Louis, his former employe, and the animal was the son of Elmer, Paul Bunyan's moose terrier. In the goodness of his heart Paul consented to act as Poissin's attorney, and at Paul's order Johnny Inkslinger had prepared the masterly brief which has been quoted in every north country dog case since.

The record of the most celebrated action at law ever undertaken in the north country is tucked away in the Chippewa County building files at Sault Ste. Marie. The certification of the case is as follows:

I, Mark W. Smith, Justice of the Peace, before whom the cause of Poissin vs. La Fave was tried, do certify to the County Court of Chippewa that the said cause was commenced on the 25th day of April, A.D. 1877, by the filing of the following declaration:

United States of North America,
State of Michigan   ⎱ss.   Before His Honor,
County of Chippewa   ⎰   Mark W. Smith:

On this 25th day of the month of April, in the year of the nativity of Jesus Christ the one thousand eight hundred and seventy-seventh (1877 as by Archbishop Usher his Computation, although there be thirty-six (36) conjectures amongst Christian chronologists on this one point alone), cometh before His Honor Mark W. Smith, one of the Justices of the Peace for the aforesaid County and much esteemed of the quality of Justice, Louis Poissin, erroneously called Possen, which by interpretation is Fish: "Quod facit per alium, facit per se," to-wit: and Paul Bunyan, logger and lumberman, citizen at least part time of Upper Michigan.

Whereas, he, the said Louis, commonly called Fish, esteemeth the said Paul Bunyan a counsel learned in the law, abounding in common sense, and outstanding in his desire to see even-handed justice dispensed in the said cause, and being possessed of abilities sufficient for the management of this case; therefore, through him, the said attorney Paul Bunyan et cetera, to the Justice aforesaid complaineth, that,

Whereas, heretofore, to-wit, on the fifteenth day of April in the said year of the nativity of Christ as aforesaid, at Sault Ste. Marie, in the County and State aforesaid, one Auguste, whose surname is James, not having the fear of God before his eyes, but being moved and seduced by the instigation of the Devil— from whose temptations may we all be delivered—in and upon the body of a certain venerable and respected Dog called Tigre, or, in the vernacular, Tiger, the property of the said Louis, commonly called Fish, then and there, wilfully, maliciously and with force and arms with malice aforethought did make an assault in most devilish and unprovoked fashion on him, to-wit, the said Tiger; the aforesaid Tigre, (Tiger in the vernacular) being of the value of Fifty Dollars ($50) lawful money of the United States of North America as aforesaid, contrary to the Peace of God and the dignity of the People of the State of Michigan;

And the said Louis, commonly called Fish, by his attorney as aforesaid, continueth his plaint and saith that the said Auguste, whose surname is James, with a certain gun, rifle, musket or pistol of the value of Twenty Dollars ($20) then and there loaded and charged with gunpowder, air and gun cotton, and with one or more leaden bullets, slugs and buckshot—which gun, rifle, musket or pistol he, the said Auguste, whose surname is James or who is sometimes so called, in his right hand then and there had and held to, against and upon the said venerable Dog Tigre (in the vernacular Tiger); and then and there wilfully and of his malice aforethought, did shoot and discharge the said lethal weapon.

And that the said Auguste, sometimes called James, with the leaden bullets, slugs and buckshot aforesaid, out of the gun, rifle, musket or pistol with malice employed upon the body of the said Tiger, then and there by force of the gunpowder and shot propelled as herein before set forth, did foully and with devilish malice discharge upon the body of the said Dog Tiger, and in and upon the head, tail, back, belly, midriff, joints, marrow and fundament of the said Tiger; that he then and there, wilfully and maliciously, did cause the said shot to strike and penetrate the wounds inflicted upon the said Dog Tiger; then and there with the leaden bullets aforesaid; so that the shot herein mentioned was discharged and sent forth from said gun, rifle, musket or pistol, by the said Auguste sometimes called James, in and upon the head, tail, back, belly, midriff, joints, marrow and fundament of him, the said Dog Tiger, causing six mortal wounds of the breadth of two inches and the depth of ten inches; of which said mortal wounds the said Dog Tiger, from the said fifteenth (15th) day of April, in the year aforesaid, until the second hour after he suffered the infliction of the same in the day, month and year aforesaid did languish, and languishing, did live; and on the day, month and year aforesaid, the said Dog Tiger, in the County aforesaid, of the said mortal wounds, while languishing, did die.

And the said Louis, commonly called Fish, of the said Auguste, whose surname is James, by his attorney aforesaid complaineth and in this wise saith: that at the time and place aforesaid, to-wit, on the fifteenth (15th) day of April, in the year aforesaid, at Sault Ste. Marie, in the County aforesaid, when foul death was done upon the body of the said venerable dog, Tigre, in the varnacular Tiger, by the aforesaid leaden bullets, slugs and buckshot, by the said gunpowder from the said gun, musket, rifle or pistol, held in the right hand as aforesaid, of him, the said Auguste whose surname is James, he, to-wit, the Dog Tigre (in the vernacular Tiger), and for many years before his death, as aforesaid upon his body was done, was of great value, use, ornament, worth, price, import and consideration to the said Louis, commonly called Fish, for the purposes, aims, ends and objects of guarding and watching the premises, domicile, castellum, dormitory, hospitium and drinken of him the said Louis commonly called Fish;

Also of drawing, hauling, and by leather harness impelling many traines de gleaset, carioles, voitures, sleds, go-carts and vehicles; also of procreating and the generation or begetting of dogs and puppies to the delectation, consolement and satisfaction of divers female dogs, sluts and bitches, all to the damage of the said Louis, commonly called Fish, of the aforesaid sum of Fifty Dollars ($50), lawful money as aforesaid.

And the said Louis, commonly called Fish, by his said attorney further saith that for the avoidance of litigation he is willing to accept the sum of Twenty-Five Dollars ($25), for that he hath suffered damages to that amount and more, by the said death done as aforesaid upon the said Dog Tiger by the said Auguste whose surname is James. Wherefore he brings suit against the said Auguste, by his attorney, Paul Bunyan.

And on the said 15th day of April, upon the filing of the action, a summons was issued returnable on the 25th day of April, A. D. 1877, at 2 o'clock in the afternoon. Personally served by John Gurnoe, Constable, continues the record.

On the above date the parties appeared and joined issue. Plaintiff declared in action of trespass on the case, through his attorney, Mr. Paul Bunyan. Defendant pleaded the general issue through his attorney and made no offer of the amount he would pay when asked by the court if he would settle without a trial.

The plaintiff demanded a jury trial and paid the requisite fee. A venire was issued for John Halloran, William Stafford, Miller Wood, Edward Ashmun, Simon C. Teeple and Alexander Bovair.

The jury was sworn. The following persons took the oath and testified on the part of the plaintiff: Hiram Lyon, Antoine Piquette, James O'Connell, George Barry, and Louis Leadbeauch.

In the temporary absence of the Clerk, the charge was read by Mr. Paul Bunyan as attorney for the plaintiff, with profound effect.

Whereupon Mr. Bunyan placed the charge in the Court's hands for filing in due course, and addressed the jury as follows:

"Gentlemen of the jury, no man can have a better or more faithful friend than his dog. There is no love more perfect, more enduring, than the mutual affection between the owner and his dog.

"You learn today that such a friendship has been foully ended. The complainant, Louis Poissin, has lost by evil means the noble animal who loved him—his chum, his pal, his playful ally; yes, the friend of his bosom, a comrade tried and true.

"Gentlemen, I am sure that you, too, have dog friends of your own, your playfellows in comradeship, your eager guardians in danger. How the eyes of such a friend light up when you return after long absence! With what transports of delight are you greeted by this jolly fellow who loves you, and who asks nothing in return but your love and good-will!

"Can you lose such a friend without a pang in the breast, or a catch in the throat? Here was your intimate companion, who never dreamed you had a single fault, who looked upon you as perfect, who thought of you as a man thinks of a god; whose heaven was to lie at your feet and to thrill at your caress.

"No, gentlemen, you are friendly men of vision. You will believe me when I tell you that he who strikes down my dog must settle with me, for he has done me a grievous wrong. He who kills my dog pierces me to the heart, for he takes away my best and truest friend.

"Can hate assume a more frightful form than the destruction of a loving comrade? Shall such a crime go unpunished? Gentlemen, the case is in your hands. Let justice be done!"

The defendant moved a non-suit, which was over-ruled by the Court. The case was then submitted to the jury, which returned to the court room in five minutes, with the following verdict:

"Your honor, we have heard the charge as expounded by Mr. Paul Bunyan, and have listened to his plea on behalf of the plaintiff, also to defendant's case for non-suit which was not allowed.

"We, the members of the jury, find the defendant guilty, and recommend that he be shot at sunrise, hung by the neck until dead, drawn and quartered, and finally burned at the stake, for committing the awful crime of wilfully and maliciously shooting the dog Tiger, beloved property of the plaintiff, Louis Poissin, as set forth in the true charge read by our distinguished fellow-citizen, Mr. Paul Bunyan. And if there could be any other punishment fitting to apply to the inquitous guilt of the defendant, we would recommend the same to your consideration."

The foreman sat down crying, and there wasn't a dry eye in the courtroom. The Justice mopped his eyes, and even Paul Bunyan was sniffling as he rose.

"Your Honor," he said, "the defendant no doubt merits the verdict of the gentlemen of the jury, who have proved themselves mindful of the precept that we must always be kind to animals. However, my client feels disposed to temper justice with mercy, and we respectfully suggest that the Court enter judgment in favor of the plaintiff, Louis Poissin and against Auguste La Fave for fifteen dollars and cost of suit." Judgment was entered accordingly.

And when darkness fell, great inroads had been made on the shipment of five hundred barrels of beer received in old Sault Ste. Marie that morning. Down on the pier there loomed, in the waning moonlight, five forgotten barrels of flour.

16

Paul Drinks the Big Lake Dry

Bill Half-a-day, Ojibway Indian chief, who lives near L'Anse on the shore of Keweenaw Bay and is a very fine chap, knew Paul Bunyan intimately. Bill swamped for Paul two winters while Tim was running the van.

Bill said that one day years ago Paul and he walked back home to the Lake Superior shore from Rhinelander, Wisconsin, where they had been looking over some timber. The day was hot and they were tired after their walk of more than one hundred miles. At least Bill was tired.

When they reached the lake shore, he said, they lay down on the rocks and drank long and deep,—that is, Paul drank and drank, Bill, being an Indian, swallowed no more than one mouthful. An Indian drinks but little of anything when he is journeying.

Then they stretched out for a few minutes under a tree, resting and cooling off, grateful for the breeze from the lake. Pretty soon, Bill said, Paul got up and went to the lake for another drink. He got down on his stomach and drank even more deeply than before.

And then, Bill continued, Lake Superior began to shrink before his very eyes. The lake level dropped and stones at the edge of the old shore line rolled down into the lake bed. Soon Bill saw thousands of fishes writhing and flopping on the beach where the water had been.

Paul reached over still farther, the water level kept on sinking, and Paul kept on drinking. In a short time Bill could see several sunken wrecks, nearly two miles out. He tried to point them out to Paul, but Paul paid no attention. He loosened his belt, reached still lower, and drank thirstily and steadily. In less than twenty minutes he drank Lake Superior dry.

"I was like a man turned to stone," said Bill. "I couldn't lift a finger or move an eyelash. There was the big lake bed, gone plumb dry, just a great big hole five hundred miles long and a thousand feet deep. I saw a flock of steamships stranded, one or two of them away over on their sides, down on the rocky bottom. I saw ten thousand gulls flying around, looking for Lake Superior, and crying because they thought it had gone forever. I prayed to the Great Spirit, and I tried, oh, how I tried to lift my eyes to Heaven, for I thought the end of the world had come."

When Paul finished drinking the waters of Lake Superior, Bill said, he stood up looking bigger than ever and faced that hollow basin all gone dry. Then he began to do some thinking, too. He took a pinch of snuff and looked a long, long time at the lake bed. Bill could see that Paul was thinking hard.

What about the steamships, the ore freighters and the grain carriers, hundreds of them that once sailed the mighty lake? It would never do to leave them marooned in that awful pit. What would the country do for whitefish and trout? And there was the question of the international boundary line and the Canadian frontier. The situation left the country wide open to smuggling, political complications, maybe invasion.

And then, what would the light house tenders do, out there on the islands which had been turned into mountains? Could they be left to starve? How would the Isle Royale folks ever get back to civilization? What would this mean to Duluth and Superior, Sault Ste. Marie and Marquette and Ashland? Wouldn't it just about ruin them? There might be some terrible times over this.

All these thoughts rushed through Paul's mind, and Bill told Tim he was so wrought up that he could read Paul's mind like an open book. He was sure that Paul could see plainly, on thinking it over, that it would never do to leave the big lake bed dry. And so, said Bill, he filled it up again.

"And how did he fill it up?" the boys asked Bill.

"He spit the water back into the hole," said Bill, "and how did you suppose he filled it up?"

"Everybody knows that Bill Half-a-day is a smart man and a credit to the Ojibway Indian nation," says Tim. "I wouldn't doubt his word for the world, but I've wondered sometimes if he didn't fall asleep under the tree and have a bad dream.

"Maybe you'd like to know why Bill was named Half-a-day," continued Tim. "Bill says that an Indian father generally names his child with regard to something that happens about the time the baby was born. Take the name Ossawinamakee, for instance, meaning Yellow Thunder. It shows that a thunder storm with yellow rolling clouds came up about the time Ossa what's-his-name was born. Or, there's Sitting Bull. It shows that his father was throwing the bull just then, and so on. Bill's father was born at noon, and of course Bill took the family name of Half-a-day. Now isn't that interesting?

"Any oldtime lumberjack will tell you about the connection between Paul Bunyan and Lake Superior. Paul was born near the lake, and when he went away he started from the lake shore. In the end Paul went up into the sky from the south shore of Lake Superior, and he never came back. Some folks say he never will come back, but we lumberjacks know better," said Tim.

"Paul used to sit for hours on the lake shore, looking out over the water, taking snuff, chuckling sometimes, and thinking hard. When the lumberjacks saw him laughing to himself, they said that every time he laughed it cost somebody ten dollars.

"But that was just their little joke."

17

Sourdough Sam, "Stummick Robber"

Thousands of Americans come to the Upper Peninsula of Michigan in peace times each summer to enjoy the cool climate, and to see the woods where Paul Bunyan flourished.

Teachers, boys and girls are interested in the land where Hiawatha lived. Many others are eager to hear more about the famous Sourdough Sam. Most people like to eat, and Sam certainly was a wonderful cook.

Sam's pea soup was a mark of his genius and almost as celebrated as his soft-nosed non-skid sinkers. Pea Soup Lake in Delta County is named in honor of Sourdough Sam. One day the tote team was coming into camp from Gladstone with four tons of split peas. Team and sleigh broke through the ice while crossing the lake, and the peas went to the bottom, but the horses and driver escaped.

Sam knew that Johnny Inkslinger would charge up the peas to the cook camp, and he hatched a bright idea for saving them. At his suggestion Paul Bunyan ordered a lumberjack crew to build a dam across the creek outlet at the foot of the lake. When the job was done Sam ordered the 300 cookees to build dozens of bonfires, close together, all the way around the lake, which was half a mile long and a quarter of a mile wide.

The water in the lake soon began to boil, and the peas were cooked in a few hours. After that, when Sam wanted some pea soup for dinner, all the cookees had to do was to open a few faucets in the dam and draw off as much soup as needed, then heat it and put it on the tables. There was always a good supply of soup on hand, for the cookees dumped more peas into the lake from time to time and cooked them in the circle of bonfires.

Paul was proud of Sam because he handled the commissary department in such a big and efficient way. When Paul walked down Ludington Street in Escanaba or State Street in St. Ignace, folks turned their heads as he went by and said to each other:

"There goes Paul Bunyan, the big logger and lumberman. His crew is so big that his cook makes a whole lake full of pea soup at one time."

Such remarks were sweet in Paul's ears, and when he overheard them he threw his chest out and looked bigger than ever. You just can't help liking folks who tell you that you're a big shot, even if you're no more than a big bootlegger. Paul liked everybody who told him that he was the world's greatest logger, and he always admitted it.

There was one thing about Pea Soup Lake that made trouble for Sam. The soup couldn't be stirred while it was cooking, and sometimes it burned around the edges of the lake. Sam put his brain to work on the problem, and he solved it by building and launching a stern-wheel steamboat on the lake. He anchored the boat in the center of the lake, and as the wheel turned over gently it stirred the soup and prevented burning. Just to make it perfect, Sam fastened rows of salt and pepper shakers on the wheel, and every lumberjack agreed that they gave the soup exactly the right flavor.

When Paul finished logging that part of the Upper Peninsula he sold the lake to Cap Fisher, who operated a hotel in Gladstone and drew his soup from Pea Soup Lake. The delicacy made his dining room famous, and Frenchmen and others were in the habit of traveling miles in order to enjoy a bowl of Cap's pea soup.

Pea Soup Lake was a great success in summer, but not even Sourdough Sam, with all his genius, was able to keep it operating as a pea soup supply base in winter. The cookees carried pea soup daily to the woods crew in cold weather, but the men complained that it reached them frozen so solidly in the kettles that they had to blast it out. Here was a knotty problem, but Sam went into conference with Joe Kadunk, the second cook, and solved it efficiently. The cookees knew that Sam was equal to any occasion within the bounds of possibilities, and they never doubted that he was the smartest cook that ever stuck his thumb into a bowl of soup.

Sam ordered the cookees to prepare two thousand pieces of tar rope, one and a half feet long. He dipped the ropes in the soup kettles, hung them outside the kitchen until the soup froze, and dipped them again. With a few dips and freezings there was plenty of soup on each piece of rope.

Then, when the pea soup ropes had been properly prepared, the cookees bunched them and carried them to the woods crew. Each man swallowed a piece of rope and held it until the soup melted. When the boys had enjoyed their lunch, the ropes were returned to the cook camp, soaked in a carbolic acid solution to destroy the germs if any, and made ready for next day's service. Before long every man had a piece of tar rope of his own, with his name on it, and eventually each member of the woods crew was provided with a new piece of rope daily, in compliance with the rules and regulations of the State Board of Health.

There was an occasional drawback to this arrangement, but it wasn't serious. Sometimes a hungry lumberjack loosened his hold on the rope and lost it down his gullet, or he held his piece of rope longer than necessary and found a tarry flavor in his soup. But in the main Sourdough Sam's modern soup delivery service appealed to the woods crew, and as for the cookees, they admired immensely his clever scheme for handling the winter pea soup problem.

"This is the proper time to settle once for all the arguments about the origin of the term 'hot dog'," says Tim. "The lumberjacks were forever arguing the question in the sleeping camp and in the woods. Joe Kadunk and I had a rather spirited discussion of this topic once. In the middle of the argument he bit a piece out of my left ear, but he did it in a gentlemanly way, and I didn't make any fuss about it.

"When the men in the woods were working not more than three miles from the cook camp, Sourdough Sam prepared a hot lunch and sent it out to them. The woods crew had breakfast each morning about half past three, and when nine o'clock came they were hungry. So at 8 o'clock daily Sam loaded a sled with kettles of frankfurts, pea soup ropes and other good food. Sometimes the cookees hauled the sled out to the men, and sometimes Elmer, the moose terrier, hauled it. When Elmer scooted down the woods road with the morning lunch, the men gave him a weenie of two from the kettle, if he didn't stop enroute to chase a moose.

"When the weather was very cold the steam rising from Elmer and the weenies made a fog like smoke in the woods. The men watched for Elmer's coming, and the minute he was in sight they hollered: 'Here's the hot dog sled coming at last.' The name was soon given to the weenies, and since that time boiled or roasted frankfurts have been called hot dogs. It's an interesting historical fact that frankfurts were first known as hot dogs in Paul Bunyan's woods camps.

"Paul was very fond of Sam's special meat and vegetable stew, which we called mulligan. When Paul came in late from the woods on a cold night, Sam was always ready for him, and Paul was tickled when he sat down at the table with a big pan of mulligan before him.

"I remember how Paul came into camp at 10 o'clock one night—he had been running section lines in Dickinson county —and almost surprised us. Sam started to warm up the mulligan and we cookees bustled around the kitchen and helped to get Paul's supper ready. There was a shelf over the cook camp stove where Sam had put things that he wanted to have handy. When Sam's back was turned I reached up to the shelf for something, I don't remember what, and I accidentally knocked a bottle of brass polish, two cans of lye, a dozen bars of yellow washing soap and ten pounds of harness grease into the big mulligan pan that was simmering on the stove.

"I was so scared I couldn't talk, so I didn't mention the accident to Sam. I knew he would thump me if I did. He placed the piping hot mulligan before Paul, and I was sure there would be an explosion. I shook with fear when Paul grasped his mighty spoon. He was as hungry as a bear, and he swallowed plate after plate of mulligan and swore that he had never tasted mulligan that was half as good. He gave Sam a big raise in salary on the spot, but although Sam tried his best, he never again succeeded in making a mulligan stew with so delicious a flavor.

"The 27th of May was Paul's birthday and we always celebrated it with a party. I recollect that in '83 the party was held about the time we finished the spring drive down the Big Auger and through the Little Gimlet Creek to the Pink Onion River, near Pollywog Lake.

"There was a big attendance of friends from Grand Marais, Newberry, Whitefish Point, Swedetown and Paradise creek. The dinner table was so long that Paul arranged a miniature railroad along the center, and it carried the salt and pepper shakers and vinegar cruets from guest to guest. All hands agreed that nothing more classy could be found anywhere, and that Paul was a great man.

"Sourdough Sam, probably thinking of his great success at Pea Soup Lake, had dammed a branch of the Pink Onion River which flowed past the camp door. He rolled half a dozen hot stones into the pool, added flour and meat stock and seasoning, and soon he had a nice supply of grand gravy. Then he ordered the cookees to pump the gravy into a water tank which we used to sprinkle the ice roads in winter.

"The tank was on an incline and off balance, and the load of gravy tipped it over. The hot gravy spilled into the timber beside the road, and the woods fire that followed burned the ground clean almost to Seney. Miles of timber went up in smoke and flame, but Paul saved the forest north of Seney by taking off his boots and carrying water in them from Pollywog lake to the scene of the fire.

"Paul docked Sam one month's pay and gave him a trimming because the gravy was spilled through his orders. 'You've never heard of my starting a woods fire,' said Paul. 'I'm careful with fire wherever I go in timber. Do you realize, Sam, that a minute's carelessness on your part has cost someone thousands of dollars? Do you think that timber grows overnight? Do you know that you passed sentence of death on thousands of fish and game when you started that fire? This time you have been no credit to the Paul Bunyan organization, and considering your years of experience in the woods, you should have known better.'

"Paul didn't fire Sam. He said Sam was too valuable a man to lose, and the lumberjacks agreed with him.

"The blaze in the Seney marshes calls to mind the fire which swept a part of the Tahquamenon swamp the same year," continued Tim. "Paul was operating a pulp wood camp in the swamp when a big fish hawk carried away a pile of 90-foot tamarack logs, which the loading crew had stacked on the river bank to be used for Lake Superior bean poles in the following spring.

"The hawk built her nest with the poles in a bog pivot pine that was the tallest tree for miles around. The nest was so close to the sun that it caught fire, and in a twinkling a wall of smoke and flame was racing across the swamp.

"We lumberjacks thought the swamp timber was doomed, but Paul saved the day with that great brain of his. He rushed Babe out of the barn and down to the river, and the big ox drank his fill. Then Paul kicked Babe in the ribs, and Babe belched just once and put out the fire.

"There's nothing like keeping your head and thinking things out when you get into a jam, and then acting without delay. It was that factor above all others that made Paul Bunyan a great man," said Tim.

18

The Pivot Hotel

In Paul Bunyan's time travel across the Tahquamenon River was heavy. Much land was being cleared, settlers were coming in, and the logging railway from the Big Falls down to Shelldrake was busy. Paul decided to build a hotel on the river bank near the railroad bridge, to house the growing transient and resorting trade, and his lumberjacks when occasion required.

The Pivot Hotel was a marvelous affair. Hotel directories gave it a Double A plus AAAA-1 rating. It had eight thousand rooms and sixteen thousand baths, so that guests registering two in a room need not wait when they wanted a bath. There were also sixteen thousand monogrammed chamber pots, just in case anything happened to the plumbing. The lumberjacks called them thunder mugs.

Why was it called the Pivot Hotel? That's a remarkable story. You see, Paul knew that practically every traveler wants a front room. In order to give his guests the best possible service, he built the hotel on a large turntable or pivot, and thus he provided front rooms for all who sojourned there. When the front rooms were sold out Paul turned the hotel around and kept right on selling front rooms.

The hotel folder issued by Paul, magnificent as it was in fourteen colors, failed adequately to describe the Pivot. The hotel had an atmosphere that was all its own, and you can't put that in a folder. All there is room for here is a few highlights of the world's greatest summer and winter, spring and fall hotel.

The distance from the lobby to the dining room was so great that guests went to their meals on a special passenger train of twenty-five cars. The three hundred cookees were mounted on roller skates, and they acted as waiters in the big dining room. They hauled the flapjacks into the dining room on flat cars, and an electric crane loaded the cars in the kitchen.

Sourdough Sam was the chef, of course, and Joe Kadunk

was assistant chef. Under their jurisdiction were fifty salad chefs, ninety pastry cooks, two hundred bakers, twenty men sorting toothpicks, and ten keepers of the finger bowls. Sam left the petty details of his big job to others, but he fried the flapjacks and boiled the pea soup himself. He said that second class flapjacks and burnt pea soup had ruined some of the largest hotels in the country, and that as for him, he wasn't going to take any chances, and that his reputation as an artist was at stake.

The flapjack griddle in the Pivot Hotel kitchen was forty-five feet in diameter, and every inch of it was under the perfect control of Sam's big combination fly swatter and pancake turner. But no piece of fat pork, however large, could grease so huge a griddle, so Sam hired sixty colored gentlemen, and they strapped hams to their feet and greased the griddle by skating over it.

At first the syrup supply for the flapjacks was a problem. Eventually Paul placed a standing order with the refiners for the delivery each week of forty tank cars of syrup and New Orleans molasses. The syrup and molasses were pumped from the cars through six-inch pipes to a row of tanks in the kitchen, and each tank was equipped with one dozen spigots of solid silver.

Paul was the first man to discover a use for white elephants. No one knew what to do with a white elephant until Paul installed ten of them in the Pivot Hotel dining room, where they were hitched to wagons and went from table to table distributing toothpicks. The white elephant stunt was a great publicity feature for the Pivot Hotel. Just about everyone would be thrilled if a white elephant happened along and passed him a toothpick. They're still talking about the toothpick wagons in the Lake Superior country.

There was a fish pond with a diameter of three hundred feet in the hotel lobby. Poles, lines, hooks, flies and spinners were standard equipment in a case on the wall of every sleeping room, and fishing privileges were included in the hotel's service to guests.

The pond was kept well stocked with the native game fish of the northland—rainbow trout, great northern pike, large-mouth and small-mouth black bass, wall-eyed pike, muskellunge,

Mackinaw trout, brown trout, whitefish, bluegills and jumbo perch. Big gamey fellows fought for a chance to be hooked, and guests could have their pick of many varieties in the clear and sparkling waters of the pool.

The moment a fish was landed a hotel photographer took shots of the angler and his trophy. The fish was planked for dinner by Sourdough Sam, and Paul Bunyan himself autographed the print for the lucky fisherman. That's just one reason why so many people have remarked since that they can't find hotel service anywhere that compares with the delights, the comforts and the thrills of the grand old Pivot Hotel.

"Naturally some small drawbacks were bound to occur in the operation of a huge hotel like the Pivot," remarks Truthful Tim. "I remember how I rode into the dining room one morning during my vacation and ordered lamb chops for breakfast. Possibly I had forgotten the immense size of the dining room and the distance from the kitchen; for while Sourdough Sam assured me later that he selected some nice tender lamb chops for me that morning, they were mutton chops when they reached my table.

"Many's the time I've gone to bed in a Pivot Hotel choice front room facing northward toward the falls and Lake Superior. As I fell asleep a cool and delightful breeze wandered off the lake and the river through the open windows," continued Tim. "But when I awoke next morning and found the early sunshine in my eyes, I knew that Chris Crosshaul, or Forty Jones, the walking boss, had brought another crew of lumberjacks into the hotel during the night, or perhaps that the Elks were holding their annual national convention at the Pivot. I realized that Paul had turned the hotel around so that every morning incoming guest could have a cool and airy front room—at front room rates, of course."

The Pivot Hotel kitchen was the show place of the house, with ample room for cooks, cookees and helpers to the total number of more than six hundred hands. Sourdough Sam was walking on air in the new quarters. He said that at last justice had been done him, and he insisted that all hands address him and refer to him as the chef. But as business increased and more and more guests were lured northward by the growing fame of the Pivot Hotel, Sam became fretful under the strain of his huge responsibilities.

Sam said that while he could handle the job of chef all right, there were some things he didn't like about the culinary department of such a big hotel. The lumberjacks who called for non-roll knives when eating their peas, and the guests who ordered caviar sandwiches and paprika salads were especially scorned by Sam. In a fit of bad temper one day he fired the colored gentlemen, who had been working like tigers skating over the big griddle and doing their best to keep it properly greased. The time was June, and flies were plentiful. Sam fished out his can of snuff and thought long and hard. Then he had an inspiration.

The tail of Babe, the Big Blue Ox, was almost forty feet long. Sam resolved to put it to work earning some money for the hotel. He brought Babe into the kitchen one morning and tied a thirty-pound skinned ham to his tail. The flies were thick and Babe's tail was working overtime. Sam gee-ed and haw-ed Babe around and backed him up until his tail swept every part of the griddle with the ham. The plan worked perfectly for two days, and Sam was sure that the commissary department would have a handsomer profit than ever on Johnny Inkslinger's books.

At 8:45 o'clock on the third morning, however, the demand for flapjacks being at the peak, Sam didn't duck quickly enough when the ham came over. It smacked him on the ear and knocked him through an open window into the river. The very first thing he did when the cookees pulled him out of the river was to kick Babe out of the kitchen. Then he put the colored gentlemen, who had been shooting craps on the rear porch, back on the job of greasing the griddle.

There were two band stands on the grounds of the Pivot Hotel, one for the orchestra of sixty pieces and the other for a band of ninety pieces. The moment one stopped playing, the other began to play. Paul's favorite selection was "Moonshine and Roses." It was soft and dreamy and shivery-like, and Paul instructed the band and orchestra leaders to play it twenty times every evening after dinner. Sometimes when Paul was in a musical mood he accompanied the combined orchestra and band with his saxophone or accordion.

"Never again do I expect to hear music like that," said Truthful Tim sorrowfully. "And I wish you could have seen the fifty swimming pools that Paul built in the front yard of the Pivot Hotel. Each pool was fifty feet square and placed on top of a big white pine stump that was hollowed out and filled with running water—hot, cold, warm or cool as desired. There was a swimming pool to please everybody. Service? You've said it, brother; we'll never, never see service like that again."

Tim added that he had been around a good deal, as far as Saginaw and North Bay, anyway, and had put up at a lot of good hotels, but he had never heard of anything in the modern world that measured up to the appointments and conveniences of the Pivot Hotel which flourished so grandly years ago in the Tahquamenon river valley.

For example, he said, the room telephone ear-pieces were built into the pillows, making it unnecessary for guests to get up or even reach out of bed when answering telephone calls. Each room was sprayed with attar of roses daily, and each had a combination shower and plunge bath, an indoor golf course and a ping-pong set.

If the guest wished to reduce or to gain weight while sleeping, all he had to do was to adjust a dial at the head of the bed before going to dreamland. This clever electrical device was the invention of Paul Bunyan. A polished plate in each room was a televisor, in which the beholder could see what was going on in any part of the world.

Another machine sterilized and delicately burnished the false teeth of guests while they slept. If the room occupant preferred to wear socks in bed, as many lumberjacks do, he could choose from six pairs of light and heavy woolen socks hanging at the foot of every bed. There were many other gadgets and improvements which, with the foregoing, made the Pivot the one perfect hotel of the ages.

"I heard of only one complaint of poor service in all the years the Pivot Hotel flourished," said Truthful Tim, "and that was when the hotel was opening and a few details were still incomplete. It happened as the result of a bartender's joke on a traveling man.

"This man had come from Chicago to the north country to sell Paul Bunyan a grocery shipment for the hotel and the camps. We could see that he was just another tenderfoot—a timid city guy who had never even smelled wood smoke until he visited the Lake Superior country. We knew that he was one of those city dumb-bells who actually can't tell a male from a female tree—something that a real lumberjack can show you in the dark, with his eyes shut. You wouldn't think it possible, but there really are folks as dumb and uneducated as that.

"This man from the big city thought that all lumberjacks were monsters instead of being the finest poeple in the world. He didn't know that we lumberjacks might scare a visitor to death, but we'd never kill him," Tim continued.

"The salesman arrived about noon and gum-shoed into the dining room as quietly as a lamb. He had a rather scared look, as if he thought his life was in danger. Paul was out in the bush that day, and after lunch the traveling man went into the bar room, where five or six bartenders were on duty. A stranger might have thought they were busy, but if he wanted to see real traffic in wet goods he could have dropped in any evening and found 60 bartenders at work, and every one of them a star.

"The drummer tiptoed to the bar and said to one of the bartenders very politely and with a catch in his voice: 'Pardon me, my dear sir, but if it isn't too much trouble, and if you can spare the time, would you mind telling me where the toilet is?'

"This kind of an approach was new to the bartender, whose name was Jack. He sized up the guest with a cold look, stuck his thumb over his shoulder and growled: 'Out there, and can't you see I'm busy?' Then he winked at a customer. The new plumbing fixtures were not yet installed.

"The salesman humbly thanked Jack and went out the back door. Presently he came back, stood around a few moments and edged over to Jack. 'Pardon me, sir,' he said in trembling tones, 'but I couldn't find the toilet.' Jack glared at him and asked loudly: 'Say you, where's your eyes? Come with me and I'll show you the toilet!'

"He grabbed the poor traveling man's arm tightly and led him to the back yard where the pine trees were thickest. 'There it is,' he said, pointing into the woods where a pole was nailed across from one tree to another, about knee-high. 'Ah,' said the traveler, 'so that's it,' and Jack replied: 'Yes, that's it, and I don't want to hear any more from you, either.' He winked at the others who were enjoying the fun. The pole was part of an old fence running through the woods.

"The man from the city stepped over, unbuttoned his galluses, and sat down carefully on the woodland 'toilet.' He had his misgivings, but then, wasn't this the wild and wooly north country? Jack had looked like an honest man. Maybe he was a jewel in the rough. It was a time for tact and forbearance, and anyway, one could see that the building was new and incomplete.

"It was a sparkling June day, too; perfect—barring some thousands of mosquitos. The sunbeams danced in the crystalline air, a fleecy cloud here and there made the blue sky seem bluer, and the soaring pines were never greener or more restful to the eye. Birds were singing all around, and the visitor could hear from afar the roar—it was muffled by the woods—of the big falls in the Tahquamenon river.

"As he sat there he fell to thinking of the beauty, the charm, the appeal of this fair north country. It really wasn't such a terrible place after all. There must be many wolves and bears in the surrounding woods. But ravenous as they must be, they wouldn't dare to venture on to the Pivot Hotel grounds. Or would they? He shivered a little as he thought of his exposed position. If a wolf attacked him on his woodland throne, he'd have to run for the hotel, that's all.

"So the man from Chicago sat on the fence, and as he mused he slapped mosquitos fore and aft. Just then down the path from the barn came One-Eye LaRue, the barn boss, who loved a joke as well as any other man. He glanced to the right and spied the traveling man sitting peacefully on his greenwood toilet, filled with admiration for the beauteous northland and keeping an eye open for bears.

"One-Eye halted, transfixed with astonishment. The thing was too complex for him. He took a pinch of snuff, pulled himself together, stepped off the path and touched the tenderfoot on the shoulder. 'What are you doing here, pardner?' he asked, and his voice and face were stern. The traveler looked up at One-Eye with deep concern. 'Why, one of the bartenders sent me out here,' he said. 'Oh, ho,' One-Eye replied, 'a bartender sent you out here, did he? And did he tell you that you're a-breaking the first rule of north country etiquette and good form? Did he? Do you know, pardner, that there's going to be hell to pay when the boss sees you a-settin' where you are a-settin'?'

" ' Why no,' the traveler stammered, starting to get up. 'I didn't know I was breaking any rules. What have I done?' 'That's all right, pardner, that's all right,' said One-Eye, cold as ice, 'but do you realize, I say, do you realize that you've been a-settin' on the ladies' side of that there twilight?' And with that the visitor fainted dead away and fell across the pole.

"Being a city man and not having a very strong constitution, it took some time for us revive him," said Tim. "He left the same day, refusing to wait for Paul's return, and he never came back. I heard later that he filed charges of mistreatment with Lansing and aired his grievance in the Chicago papers. Probably he never learned that some of Paul Bunyan's lumberjacks had been spoofing him."

The day came when the virgin pine stand in the Tahquamenon Falls country was exhausted, and the Pivot Hotel closed its doors for the first and last time. The Pivot had been a good investment and Paul dismantled it with regret. He sold the lumber and the fixtures to the highest bidders, and presented the white elephants to the King of Siam, a country where many people keep white elephants to run errands and help with the chores.

A man from Cheboygan bought the entire stock of beautiful hand painted monogrammed china thunder mugs. He sold a boatload of them to the Grand Hotel on Mackinac Island. Later, when the Grand installed toilets throughout, he bought them back and sold them to northern Michigan farmers. Today they repose in many farm houses in the northern part of the Lower Peninsula, precious relics of the great and only Pivot Hotel.

All that is left of the Pivot is a clearing beside the river, above the big falls. Possibly a second growth of timber has covered the clearing by this time. Paul and his crews moved on to other timber limits needed for the great job of housing the growing central west and the Mississippi valley.

The change back to normalcy suited most of the lumberjacks. They allowed that they weren't used to such grandeur, but a few of the boys groused and grumbled. A couple of years afterward Paul built his celebrated "Uplift Camp" to please the malcontents. It is worthy of a later chapter.

19

Paul's Logging Railroad

"Shortly after Paul Bunyan got a good start in the logging industry he built the world's most remarkable logging railway through the Upper Peninsula woods," said Truthful Tim.

"The deep water terminal of Paul's railway was at Shelldrake on the shore of Whitefish Bay, an arm of Lake Superior. The line stretched westward through heavy timber and the Paradise country, past the Pivot Hotel, to the Tahquamenon River and beyond. It was known far and wide as Paul Bunyan's Side-Hill Railway, and parts of the old bridge across the Tahquamenon, and of the right of way through Paradise, are still visible.

"I was a member of the crew that cleared the right of way and graded Paul's side-hill line. We cut down no hills and filled up no valleys along the route. If there was a forty per cent grade over a hill, we graded it, and if a valley was a couple of hundred feet deep, with a sink-hole in the bottom of it, we graded that.

"In some places where we laid rails around or across the side of a hill, one rail would be two feet higher than the other. Folks stood around and laughed themselves sick when they saw the road bed. They said no train could ever run on a road like that. But Paul fooled 'em. He put a gyroscope on the engine and on each flat car, and we never had even a single derailment in more than twelve years of the line's operation, although trains often ran at speeds of over one hundred miles an hour.

"At the beginning we used a small Lima locomotive—the lumberjacks called it a dinky—on his side hill line. Paul owned up afterward that he made a mistake in buying the dinky. It was so small that he couldn't get into the cab, and there wasn't room enough for him even after he had taken off the cab roof.

"We solved that problem by providing a special flat car for Paul when he was bossing woods operations along the line. The old Lima turned up in the end at Ontonagon, and I heard that the Ontonagon Civic League planned to place it on view in the community park as a Paul Bunyan memorial.

"Paul had another Lima engine that was worth seeing. Its cylinders were both on the right side, cog wheel style, and the driving wheels were not much larger than saucers. Paul gave this dinky to Al Paulson at Osceola, and it is the star piece in Al's museum. I've spit over it many a time.

"But these kettles weren't what Paul wanted. They hauled only four loads at a time and their overhead was too great. He ordered Johnny Inkslinger to draw plans for a real locomotive. Now Johnny had been an engineer before he reformed and resolved to lead a better life, and came north to keep the books for Paul Bunyan. He planned and built a locomotive for Paul that was so blamed big that it had twelve sets of hinges on the boiler, so it could go around the sharpest curves. Johnny installed a mammoth gyroscope on it, and on the very first trip out of the woods the monster hauled two thousand and fifty cars of logs down to the Shelldrake terminal. When the engine was passing the Shelldrake banking grounds the caboose was actually seven miles back in the timber. You can see from that what a powerful machine it was.

"Maybe you've heard about this famous locomotive. It was so big that the six firemen used motorcycles to run around the thing when they were oiling it up in the morning. When it was hauling a capacity tonnage out in the hills, it passed the caboose on its own train twenty-seven times while rounding the curves.

"The same engine holds the world's speed record to this day. With Paul Bunyan himself at the throttle, and reporters and photographers from the leading railway journals in the cab and hanging on for dear life at the rear end of the caboose, it traveled at the rate of two hundred and ninety miles an hour on a measured stretch of ten miles. Following this run the entire ten miles of track had to be rebuilt. The engine's speed was so great that in some places the track curled up into knots behind it, and one section tore loose and stood a mile high in the air.

"So many settlers took up homesteads along Paul's line that Paul bought an old passenger car for their accommodation in getting out to Shelldrake and Newberry. He raised the roof so he could walk down the aisle without stooping, and hitched the car on the daily logging train, behind the caboose.

"Paul liked to take up tickets in the coach. He ordered a blue cap from his tailor, and on the front of it were these words in gold letters:

THE PAUL BUNYAN LOGGING RAILROAD
PAUL BUNYAN
CHAIRMAN OF THE BOARD,
PRESIDENT,
GENERAL MANAGER,
SUPERINTENDENT,
ALSO THE CONDUCTOR

"Some of the settlers thought that Paul was the world's greatest railway executive. Others allowed that he was kidding himself.

"One day the train was rolling down to Shelldrake, hell bent for Wednesday, over hills and around the curves, and Paul was punching tickets in the coach. A woman gave him a half fare ticket for her boy. Paul looked the boy over and said to the woman: 'Now, missus, I can't carry this boy on a half-fare ticket. Why, you can see for yourself that he's wearing long pants!'

" 'All right, Mr. Bunyan,' said the woman, 'if that's the way you figure it, let him ride on my ticket and I'll travel on the half-fare ticket.'

"This put Paul up a tree and out on a limb for a minute, and he didn't know what to say, if anything. While he was reaching for his can of snuff and trying to do some hard thinking, a woman sitting across the aisle spoke up. 'Mr. Bunyan,' she said, 'if that's how it is, I shouldn't be paying any fare at all!'

"Sniffy McGurk was the brakeman that trip, and he said Paul was so flustered that he let more than a dozen people ride free into Shelldrake, for he clean forgot to take up their fares. And that night he got tight on some bottles of bitters that he had been saving up for Christmas.

20

Paul Goes Fishing

"Fishing is always a delicate subject, requiring high-souled integrity on the one hand, and faith and confidence on the other.

"Many's the time I've gone fishing with Paul Bunyan," continues Truthful Tim, "but unlike some fishermen, I propose to stick to the facts, in line with Paul's constant advice and counsel. And if you doubt what I'm telling you, ask Harry Mertins of Iron River or Harold Lindsay of Escanaba whether it's the honest northern Michigan truth. They've fished with Paul, too.

"I remember a traveling preacher who sometimes came to camp over the week-end. Once he preached to us in the cook camp dining room, where there was plenty of room for benches. His subject was Jonah and the whale. He told how Jonah had lived for seven days and eight or nine nights in the whale's belly. Paul couldn't believe it—he just knew it couldn't be done, but he was too polite to interrupt the preacher. And besides, Paul wasn't up on theology and he had never heard of Jonah.

"After the services Paul took the preacher aside and asked him as a personal favor not to tell the boys any more tall tales like the Jonah story. He said he didn't want his lumberjacks to get the habit of telling fish stories that would possibly stretch the honest truth to the breaking point.

"Paul was a truthful man, and he couldn't bear to have anyone near him who wasn't careful with the facts. Today, the good effects of Paul's firm stand for the truth can be seen all over the Upper Peninsula of Michigan, where an untruthful man or woman is shunned as if he or she had been guilty of telling a cock and bull story about a whale.

"Paul told me he had a strange experience one summer when fishing in the Dead River near Negaunee," continued Tim. "He had left camp in a hurry that morning, and when he came to the first fishing hole and unlimbered his tackle, he found he was wearing the wrong hat, with no flies stuck in the band.

"While he was cussing himself and wondering what to do, he

said, he spied a six-foot pine snake with a frog in its mouth. So he cut a forked stick, put it gently over the snake's head, and took the frog away from it. Paul said he was grateful to the snake for bringing him some bait, and he didn't kill it as some fishermen might have done. He let it go, but first, by way of regard for the frog, he gave the snake a little tot of pain killer that he carried on his hip in case of a sprained ankle or a shower.

"In less than a minute Paul caught a fine big speckled trout with the only frog he had, and the trout swallowed the frog. The question arose—should he mangle the fish, or go back to camp with only one trout? He dipped some snoos and scratched his head, and he was thinking mighty hard, he said, when he heard a thump, thump, on a log beside him. There was the pine snake, looking up at Paul with the friendliest expression, wagging its tail and carrying another frog in its mouth.

"Paul told the boys that he was simply speechless with surprise and appreciation. Never in his life had he seen such gratitude from a poor dumb animal. He took the frog, gave the snake another little snort from the bottle, and the snake went after another frog. Working co-operatively, they finished the quart, the snake brought in twenty-six frogs, and Paul went back to camp with twenty-six fine fish, taking the pine snake with him for a pet. Paul named the snake Bucyrus, after the steam shovel used on the woods roads. He and Bucyrus were pals for years and they often went fishing together. This story teaches us that it pays to be kind to animals, even snakes.

"Speaking of snakes, I've lived more than half a century in the Upper Peninsula of Michigan, cookeeing, swamping, decking, bushing, and running vans for Paul, but I've never seen a snow snake. I've heard folks say that the peninsula was full of snow snakes at one time, but in my opinion the snow snake existed only in the minds of certain people who were not overcareful with the truth," Tim went on.

"Paul was fond of animals, kind and patient with them, and he got some remarkable results in teaching them tricks. His educated fishworm, Julius Caesar, was an example of his skill with animals. I have never seen Julius Caesar perform, but my uncle had a cousin whose sister's father-in-law was distantly related to the foster-brother of a man who used to work for Paul Bunyan's Aunt Susie, and he knew a man who had often seen Julius Caesar.

"Julius could count from one to seventeen and he played a very fair game of cribbage. The lumberjacks taught him to chew Peerless, and he enjoyed a pinch of snuff morning and evening. But it was Paul who taught Julius how to fish. When Paul went fishing on Lake Superior with Julius he seldom used a hook. He dropped his line into the lake, pushed Julius overboard, and Julius crawled down the line and proceeded to fish. He just loved to fish.

"Julius would lay in wait near the bottom of the lake and suddenly take a strangle hold on a forty-pound trout. Then he grabbed the line and gave Paul the signal to pull up. They often caught a ton or more of fish a day that way.

"Once, my uncle said, Julius tackled a sturgeon that must have weighed a couple of hundred pounds, and the sturgeon put up a terrible fight. It almost got away, but Julius subdued it by jabbing his tail into the fish's eye. The lumberjacks were sure that Julius enjoyed revenging himself while fishing, and that he was getting even with the fish because they had eaten so many of his brother fish-worms.

"Paul said he knew more than thirty ways to catch fish. Sometimes he rowed far out on Lake Superior, searching for schools of Mackinaw trout and whitefish, in what he called his small flatboat. It was only five hundred feet long and a couple of hundred feet wide. When he discovered a large school, he rowed directly over it and made a noise like a schoolmaster. Generally the entire school of fish jumped out of the water into the boat. Two or three schools made a fish fry for the entire crew.

"Paul had another clever fishing idea. He ordered Big Ole, the blacksmith, to make a combination pike pole and canthook one hundred feet long. Taking the pole in his fishing boat, Paul speared one monster whitefish after another in the eye. Then he gave the canthook a twist and rolled the fish toward the shore at such high speed that the water soon became boiling hot. Thus the fish were caught and cooked in the combined operation, with a big saving in time and fuel.

"I never could explain an experience that Paul and I had one day at Lake Michigamme. The first fish we caught was a muskellunge. We had scales in the boat, and the muskie weighed sixty pounds. When we got back to camp the cookees dressed it and found a sturgeon in its stomach that weighed eighty-five pounds. We couldn't figure it out, but anyway the fishing was good.

"Paul's speckled trout fishing record still stands unmatched. He stood on the Fox River bridge west of Seney one morning with a fish pole sixteen miles long, and caught every speckled trout within that radius in all directions. In the next two years not a trout was landed in thirty miles of territory. This happened before Paul met Tiny, and it was she who taught him not to be a fish hog.

"We never went fishing for black bass when we were cutting the pine in the Huron Mountain country. We went hunting for them. Fish hawks were plentiful and when we wanted bass we watched the hawks. They did the fishing for large-mouth black bass in Ives and Mountain lakes and down the Yellow Dog and Salmon Trout Rivers.

"When a hawk flew up into a tree with a ten-pound bass, we nicked his claws or fanned his tail with a rifle bullet, being careful not to kill him. This scared him into dropping the fish. It took some crack shooting to avoid frightening the hawks and driving them out, and with good marksmanship we kept the hawks fishing for us all summer. We often went back to camp with all the bass we could carry, fish that we had landed with a rifle and a fish hawk or two."

21

Paul's Uplift Camp

"But I must tell you about the Paul Bunyan uplift camp, and how Paul taught his lumberjacks a lesson which they never forgot," said Truthful Tim, as he stowed away a large helping of Peerless.

"You see, after Paul dismantled the Pivot Hotel, most of the boys settled down in good old type log camps in the Upper Peninsula woods. Many of the lumberjacks had never stopped at the Pivot. Dozens of them built shacks in the great Tahquamenon swamp and boarded themselves. They said the Pivot Hotel was too toney for them and that it put on too much dog.

"But some of the men grumbled because, they said, log camps were behind the times and lacked modern comforts. They thought Paul Bunyan should lead off in new and better ideas for camps. New men joining Paul's forces made much of this idea, and all recalled the vanished glories of the Pivot Hotel.

"The traveling preacher-missionary—he was a mighty fine chap, but his foot slipped when he told us the whale story—was always telling us about the higher things and the broader vision. He said if we were patient and faithful some day we could make good, maybe, on better jobs that we could get in the bush. Somehow he never could understand that being a lumberjack is the most valuable and important job on Earth. The country could get along somehow without the clergy, but believe me, it would be sunk without its lumberjacks.

"We liked the preacher, but we could see that he was lumberjack shy—kind of careful how he rubbed against us, probably fearing that he might catch a cootie. And of course when he told us the story of Jonah and the whale it jarred all of us who had strict regard for the truth.

"This same parson almost persuaded me to enter the ministry, and I can see now that I had a mighty close call," said Tim. "I've made good as a lumberjack, and being only a clergyman would have been a terrible come-down for me. As a lumberjack I don't take anything from anybody, but I've got to admit that I wouldn't have made a red hot parson.

"When we returned to our life in log cabins, there was grumbling in camp about the food—a choice of five kinds of meat for dinner wasn't enough. Some of the boys said there ought to be not less than seven kinds of meat and sausage, with fish and eggs. Some didn't like the honey because it was served in the comb. Others said strained honey wasn't fit to eat; that it was an insult to any self-respecting lumberjack to ask him to eat strained honey, and something ought to be done about it. The eggs were either too hard or too soft. There wasn't any system in the cook camp any more; the cooks weren't on to their jobs and the cookees were a fresh lot.

"Those cookees had tried to poison some of the lumberjacks by serving turned-over eggs, when the doctor had told them particularly that they were in danger of their lives if they ate eggs cooked any other way than straight up. The coffee was sour, the jam was sour, the sinkers were sour. Whoever named Sourdough Sam the Stummick Robber knew what he was talking about. The bunks were no good, the sleeping camp was too hot, the Peerless was moldy, and the snoos, being made of sawdust, had no authority. It was a hell of a camp and nobody but a lot of white-livered rabbits would ever stay in such a place. But they all stayed.

"And then Paul announced his decision to build an uplift camp, something up to date and different, a camp that would be a model for all logging camps everywhere, Russia and Australia not excepted. He contracted with Walter Prickett of Sidnaw for the logging of twenty sections near that town in Houghton county. Walter, who was once a lumberjack and later made a fortune in iron ore, designed the uplift camp buildings that were put up in a row on the shore of Mustard Pie Lake.

"Paul said: 'I'm here to show the boys that I'm strong for uplift and culture. I am planning a woods camp that will compare favorably with the Grand Hotel on Mackinac Island; yes, that will outshine the Pivot Hotel of which we were all so proud.

" 'My new camp will be a place where the President of the United States and the Governor of Michigan and members of Congress and the Supreme Court will be delighted to spend their vacations. I foresee the day when travel will increase and thousands of people will come each summer to the cool north country woods—if I don't cut 'em all down. This new camp of ours will be the talk of the country, and it will set a high mark for the log cabin de luxe accommodations of the future.'

"Paul made a pile of money in the logging business that year, and he built the new camp regardless. He put hot and cold running water, toilets and showers and electric lights in every cabin and every room. He ordered forty tons of copper shingles from Calumet and roofed the buildings with them. Think of it, copper roofs on the cook camp and the sleeping camp, and your own room in your own cabin if you wanted one!

"Yes, each lumberjack could have his separate room, clean linen daily, and a telephone in his room for the asking. Each room had a reading lamp and a writing desk, and the desks were veneered with Escanaba birds eye maple.

"Beneath the desk lid the lumberjack found pens, pencils, blotters, a pin cushion, an individual manicure set, and one hundred letterheads of the finest bond paper. On each sheet were the printed words:

PAUL BUNYAN
THE BIG LOGGER
UPPER PENINSULA OF MICHIGAN

"Below, at the left, the lumberjack found his name printed in gold embossed letters. This feature interfered some with our woods operations until the novelty wore off. Many of the lumberjacks were on the sick list for the first two weeks. They couldn't leave their rooms for days. They had their meals served in their rooms by the three hundred cookees, and they kept me busy for hours in the van, ordering and distributing sheets of postage stamps. The boys spent most of their time in their bath robes, writing home and mother and Sears Roebuck and Montgomery Ward.

"On the bottom of the letterheads, too, was the cut of a saw log with a beaver chewing on it. Of course it meant: 'I am logging logs and I am as busy as a beaver.' Mighty clever, we thought.

"The expression, 'to spruce up,' was first used at Paul Bunyan's uplift camp. It was the greatest job of sprucing up ever done at a logging camp. Every man had orders to shave clean each morning before starting out with his ax or peavy to the woods job or to work on the loading gang. A notice was posted on the bulletin board that all hands must have their boots shined at the barber shop each day after breakfast, seven days a week. Every lumberjack was required to have his pants properly pressed before leaving camp, under pain of being reported by the inspector. Every employee, including the cookees, was ordered to have a hair cut, shampoo, massage and a Turkish bath at least once a week, with a special manicure on Saturday nights.

"Paul said he wanted to show the boys that his heart was in the right place and that he was anxious to do his bit for the higher life. He placed a standing order with a Crystal Falls florist for the delivery of two thousand carnations in camp each morning and five thousand roses on Sundays, so that every lumberjack could go to work in the woods with a posy in the buttonhole of his jumper. Paul said to us:

" 'Boys, I'm with you right up to the hilt on this move for better things and the higher life, and I'm going sled-length to make you satisfied and happy. But if I call your bid and go you one better I don't want to hear you beefing about old times and the happy days of long ago. I figure that you're going to be so grateful for what I'm doing for you that the woods cut will show an increase of at least twenty per cent, beginning this month. Efficiency is what we want, and I'm strong for anything that will make you more efficient than you ever were before.'

"Paul ordered oak floors laid in all the camps, and he assigned a valet to each lumberjack. The valet pressed the lumberjack's pants while he was sleeping, and drew his bath water in his private tub each morning,—hot, cold, or luke, as preferred, and if the lumberjack didn't fancy a shower. At the table every man

tucked a clean napkin under his chin at each meal, and the napkin
was embroidered with his initials. If he made too much noise
while inhaling his pea soup, of if he dunked a sinker in his coffee,
he was fined, and if he persisted in his evil ways he was told to
go to the office and get his time.

"As for sowbelly, no one even dared to mention it. We had
chicken and ice cream three times a day, and lettuce salad. But
no one ate the salad, as it wasn't very filling. Paul engaged a brass
band to entertain us at meal time, and he paid an expert to come
from New York and give us lessons every evening in bridge and
contract whist.

"In place of the old camp horn which Sourdough Sam had
been using to wake us up at three o'clock in the morning, Paul
put an electric call bell in every room. A notice on the bulletin
board instructed all employes to leave a call at the central office
before turning in.

"Paul said he reckoned the cook camp horn was out of date,
vulgar and obsolete. But it always sounded grand and beautiful
to me at meal time. Paul allowed that the call bells would appeal
to our better natures and bring us up smiling in the morning. He
grinned when he said it, and I guess he was kidding us.

"There was every last convenience in Paul Bunyan's uplift
camp except hired girls—some people call them maids. Paul
knew what he was doing when he left the hired girls out. Not
that a thousand hired girls wouldn't have been safe in camp; no
one ever heard of a real lumberjack who would harm a decent
woman. Even the other kind would have a better chance with
the average lumberjack than with a man from the city. I'd say
that a woman is a good deal safer in the Upper Peninsula woods
than she is on State street in Chicago, and I don't mean auto-
mobiles, either.

"Paul knew that having women in a logging camp is the same
thing as talking at the table—it always starts an argument. When
folks keep their mouths shut at the table, nobody starts anything; and when you keep away from women, or keep the women
away from you, there's no chance for trouble.

"There never was anything so fine as the Paul Bunyan uplift
camp since Adam was a yearling. Visitors who came to see it said

it was a lumberjack heaven. But two weeks after it started the lumberjacks were grumbling.

"One-Eye LaRue was the first to complain. He said he was used to a log cabin where the bore-worms in the logs could lull him to sleep at night with their boring a-going close to his ear. He said he couldn't sleep well in the new camp, it was so blamed still.

"Joe Kadunk allowed that he never could get used to the patent egg cookers which Paul had installed in the kitchen so that Sourdough Sam and he could boil three-minute eggs. He said he could time boiling eggs to the second without any new-fangled clock arrangement, and he thought it was a reflection on his cooking and Sam's when these dinguses were forced on cooks who knew their business and weren't going to stand for any mean digs about their cooking.

"Sniffy McGurk said it was no use at all trying to sleep in a feather bed with a ten-foot ceiling in the room, where you couldn't snuggle up close to the eaves and hear the rain pattering soft-like on the roof, close to your head. He said there was something downright deleterious about this here camp, and he wished he could get back into a log shack like he used to call home, and have a nice comfy time when he wasn't working out in the bush. A place where you could wiggle your toes without being thrown out, was the way he put it.

"Chris Crosshaul said it was too blasted much for him, trying to sleep in a camp where there was no line over the stove where you could hang up your wet socks and dry them out over the fire. He said he could see now that he never could be happy anywhere but in a log sleeping camp where there was a Quebec stove and a sawdust spit-box and a real straw bunk. And he wanted to sleep where there was a fire in a stove that would go out nights, natural-like, so that his socks would be frozen stiff when he got up in the morning, the way they ought to be in any camp that was a camp.

"Chris said that if he didn't have to thaw out his socks before he put them on his feet on a winter morning, he was just simply sunk for that day, and he couldn't get the work out of the men no how that Paul expected him to. He said steam radiators might be all right for city folks, but it was a sure thing they were never made to hang wet socks on. And that as for him, he was going to be a total loss if things kept up this way much longer.

"All this time, while the boys were trying to blow out the electric lights before they turned in, and torturing their immortal souls trying to learn how to play contract bridge, which the high brow from down east was having a time trying to teach us, Paul was sniggering up his sleeve. He wasn't a fool, Paul wasn't, and he knew that when the boys had enough of the higher life they would give up their fool notions about uplift and all that, and be real lumberjacks again.

"The fact was that the entire crew was slowly dying of homesickness. One day, when we couldn't stand it any longer, we signed a round robin and handed it to Paul in the office, humbly asking him to cut out the embroidery and give us a real logging camp again. Paul read it, laughed, and pulled a paper out of his pants pocket on which three words were scribbled: "I KNEW IT." When it was passed around we all agreed that Paul knew what he was doing and was wiser then we were.

"Soon we were back again in our old double-deck wood bunks, sleeping on straw pads in an old-fashioned log sleeping camp. It was floored with rough pine boards full of knot-holes —a real floor. We hung our wet socks on a line over the red hot camp stove and enjoyed the fragrance of them. They didn't smell like sweet violets, they smelled natural, like wet socks drying on a line over a hot stove ought to smell.

"We broke the ice in the water pails and soused our necks in the morning as we did in years gone by, and we raised a million oldtime goose pimples. We shaved every other week, or the last Sunday in the month, or we let the spinach grow and never shaved at all if we didn't feel like it.

"We ditched the electric lights and went back to tallow candles and lanterns and coal oil lamps. Boy, it was good to see those friendly glims again! There's something cold and hard about an electric light bulb, but there's nothing prettier in the world than the gleam of a lantern dancing along a woods road at night, with the yellow light shining on the trees and shimmying on your legs.

"And how we felt at home when Sourdough Sam dusted off the cook camp horn and called us to chow with it again! While I think of it, Sam was never known to blow down acres of timber with that horn. He was careful to point it toward the sky so that no harm would be done. Some folk have said that he knocked down four sections of timber every time he blew the horn, but such talk would never appeal to a truthful man. Sam wasn't big enough to do that and besides, he didn't have the wind.

"Johnny Inkslinger told me that long before I came to camp Paul blew the horn one night at the full moon, and that the man in the moon stood on his head for eight or nine months before he could right himself. No one doubts that Paul could do this, for he had a big chest expansion and a lot of hair on his breast. But such a feat as that was, or blowing down timber with the horn was out of the question for Sam. Anyway, when we were so hungry that our slats were knocking together, and the old horn called us to red horse and sowbelly again, we thought it made far sweeter music than any call bell.

"Soon we were back to normal. No one took a bath that winter, and no one had a cold. We ate our tobacco and spit in a corner if the spit-box wasn't handy. The cookees shipped their fish-and-soup uniforms back to the man in Detroit who rents clothes for amateur theatricals. They brought the grub to the tables in their shirt sleeves instead of tip-toeing in with individual portions of fricasseed chicken that wouldn't keep a chickadee alive. If we wanted to dunk, we dunked. And best of all, we kicked out the card sharp and went back to playing rummy and smear evenings for a penny a point, just like human beings.

"Then Paul told us that he could see from the start that the uplift, as the preacher called it, wasn't going to work out. Said he: 'Boys, I gave you what you wanted, and you didn't like it. Now we are going to chop out all this dead timber and live like real Americans again.'

"We said to him: 'Boss, thanks a lot for teaching us a lesson and for giving us a real logging camp once more.'

"You may be sure there was no more uplift or culture in Paul's camps after that, and everybody was cheerful and happy.

" 'That uplift camp was one of the best investments I ever made,' said Paul to me long afterward."

22

Babe, the Big Blue Ox

" 'Where can we find Babe, the Big Blue Ox?'

"The question is asked dozens of times each summer by tourists in the Upper Peninsula of Michigan," said Truthful Tim. "Now you must understand that Babe wasn't born blue. His hide turned blue in the winter of the blue snow that I am going to tell you about.

"Everybody knows that Babe was the biggest ox that ever lived," continued Tim. "We lumberjacks tried to measure him, but he just refused to be measured. Maybe he was ashamed of his oversize. Sniffy McGurk and I estimated that he was ten ax handles and six plugs of tobacco wide between the eyes, and that will give you some idea of his great size.

"Babe lived on cat-tails and suckers. He wouldn't work when the suckers were running the creeks. You could tell from the glint in his eyes that he had his mind on suckers, and he would go miles for a mess of them. One-Eye LaRue, the barn boss and the only man in the north country besides Paul that could handle Babe, spent much of his time hauling in cat-tails for the big ox when the sucker runs were over. Babe ate nine or ten thousand cat-tails a day when he could get them. That's a lot of cat-tails, and One-Eye said sometimes that Babe was a pernicious old reptile.

"Big Ole, the camp blacksmith, made ten sets of bull-wheels for Babe. With a pair of bull-wheels and the right kind of a chain Babe could walk off with the biggest log that ever grew in the northwoods. A beautiful pair of these wheels may be seen at the Paul Bunyan museum in Blaney Park, and there are others at the Parker Hotel and Bear Trap Lodge on the shores of Indian Lake.

"Some years ago a group of engineers built a dam across the Skunk Cabbage River, which had been flowing north into Lake Superior. Shortly after the dam was completed they found that another dam, farther up stream, would be necessary to keep the water from flowing south into Lake Michigan.

"This completely baffled the engineers, and to this day they never solved the mystery of the river that flowed up and flowed down. Any of Paul's lumberjacks could have given them the reason. What happened is easily understood by anyone except an engineer.

"Paul Bunyan drove logs and pulpwood up and down the Skunk Cabbage River for years. Generally about half the winter's cut was delivered at Lake Superior and the other half went to Lake Michigan. With Babe's aid Paul reversed the river's flow whenever he wanted to.

"When the drive was ready for his Lake Superior mill he opened the booms at the north end, and the pine floated out into the lake. Then the booms would be closed, holding maybe a million cords of pulpwood in the river. As soon as the Manistique paper mill was ready for its wood quota, Paul gave Babe a double ration of salt and led him to drink say four or five miles upstream. When Babe began to drink, the river's current reversed itself, and the pulpwood floated south to Manistique.

"After this happened a few times the river became sort of discouraged, and didn't seem to give a whoop which way it flowed. A few of the engineers made a half-hearted effort to figure it out, but they were hopeless. You see, they had no imagination. Johnny Inkslinger tried to explain what was happening, and he even drew a diagram of the operation for them, but being engineers they never were able to get a clear solution of the problem through their heads.

"Babe was in his prime about the time Paul's big lumber hookers began carrying their cargoes down Lake Huron to Detroit, Cleveland and Buffalo. Before long the Chicago dealers began calling for Paul's lumber too, but there was no way at that time for him to deliver Lake Superior lumber by water to the head of Lake Michigan.

"But Paul solved the problem. He drove Babe over to St. Ignace, which was an inland town at that time, and dug the Straits of Mackinac. Paul and Babe and the woods crew turned their attention to dredging, and they did a wonderful job. They dredged rock enough out of the channel to build Mackinac Island, the Fairy Isle, Paul called it. I suppose it is the most beautiful island in the whole world. Paul logged the mainland timber and cut the lumber for the Grand Hotel.

"The Grand is a real good hotel, sumptuous and magnificent like the Pivot Hotel was," continued Truthful Tim. "But of course the beautiful hand painted, monogrammed thundermugs, the Pride of the Pivot, are scattered to the four winds now. Furthermore, the Grand has no turntable and Mr. Woodfill can't turn it around when the front rooms are sold out.

"It's true that critics have sneered at the great work done by Paul Bunyan, Babe and the woods crew in that part of the country," said Tim. "They complain that Paul built the Straits wider than was necessary and that the cost of bridging them will be very high. But there will have to be a bridge between St. Ignace and Mackinaw City before long, and the remaining members of the Paul Bunyan Lumberjacks Association will help the Michigan State Highway Department build it, if necessary. If Paul and Babe and the good old woods crew gang were only here, there would be nothing to it. We'd build the bridge complete in sixty days."

Tim took a big pinch of snuff, and reflected. "Yes, I wouldn't be afraid to bet that we could do the job in forty-five days, provided Johnny Inkslinger could be there to draw the plans and supervise construction," he went on. "But I must tell you about Babe's weakness. He was crazy about cat-tails and suckers, of course, but he was mighty fond of rock salt, too. Years ago on a winter evening, One-Eye LaRue was leading Babe to camp through the Menominee county woods. They were walking over a high bluff, and when Babe saw ice glittering below him in the valley, he must have thought it was rock salt.

"He jerked loose and scrambled down and began to lick the ice greedily. His tongue scooped three big holes in the ground, and the following summer the holes filled with water. Babe's tongue marks are easily recognized today. The largest hole became Green Bay. Little and Big Bay de Noc were formed when his tongue slipped on the right and left sides of the ice, and of course Green Bay is the exact shape of Babe's tongue.

"If Babe had given the ice one more lick it would have made another and a shorter waterway between Lake Michigan and Lake Superior.

"Babe became blue in the Winter of the Blue Snow which astonished the people living in the Lake Superior country," said Tim. "I was pursuing my studies for the ministry in lower Michigan that winter, but years later Big Ole, the camp blacksmith, wrote me an account of it, as follows:

Deer Teem: Meenie Aplis, Meenie Sowta,

Ay tank Ay bin only lumberyack left but yu, as remember how da snow bin so blew back by ayeteen eyety vun.

Wan day, Babe, he bin get in a yam, pullin hon a beeg pine log. Dey bin ayety four of us Svedes, dirty sax Frenchman, tree Fins, and Paul (course Paul he bin Svede too, makes ayety five Svedes), all wid canthukes trying to un-yam dat beeg pine log dat bin yammed.

Babe he bin huke hon by beeg chain to pull hout dat yammed log. Bimeby he pull so hard he git yammed in mud too. Den all hands yell—"Geedhup yu dam so-and-so!" and dey yab and yerk and yolt and yar and yog heem around so he bin disyusted, and bimeby he bin yammed in mud way oop by hees belly.

Den all hands dey start to svear—Yeeroosalem, Teem, how dey svear! Lak only lumberyacks kin svear! An by da yumpin yiminy, in yoost no tam de air bin blew for miles and miles— oh, so blew as Lak Soopeerier she's blew—yoost so dam blew as da blewest blew you nefer saw.

Den da Blew Snow he's fall for 8 days and nine nights—it smear everyting blew in a yiffy. It look so yoost lak vater dat Paul he wade ayety miles out in Lak Soopeerier and he bin ofer hees boot tops before he find out vere he is at.

Oy, yaas, Teem, Ay fergit to say es day pine log as bin yammed reached from Bessemer way oop past Lak Gojeebick. Now you know 'bout da Blew Snow, Teem, yoost how she's come, hey?

Trooly,
OLE.
P.S. En Babe she's bin blew hall tam since.

23

The Great Pole-sitting Contest

According to Tim, Ole's log had a remarkable history. It was in the Winter of the Blue Snow that astronomers in Greenwich and Washington announced their computations, showing that the exact center of the Universe is in Hermansville, Menominee county, in the Upper Peninsula of Michigan. The Hermansville community club house is built on the location.

After the blue snow melted and Babe hauled the big log out of the swamp to higher ground, Paul Bunyan sent a crew of Irish and Finn lumberjacks—Finn, not Fin as Ole said—to trim and peel the tree. Paul planned to use it as a flag pole at the universal center in Hermansville.

Then he sent another crew—they were Swedes and Frenchmen—to Hermansville, with orders to dig a hole for the flag pole at the spot named by the scientists, and to paint the pole as soon as it was delivered.

Paul was busy that week up at the Dirty Dick camp, but the project moved along smoothly until Babe, the Finns, and the Irish moved into town with the pole, and met the Frenchmen and the Swedes on this unique central spot, where, of all places in the world, peace and good will might be expected to prevail. They endured for the space of nearly thirty seconds. Then a French lumberjack yelled: "To hell with the Irish!"

The ruckus that followed almost dwarfed the American Civil War. Fists, boots, knees, heads and teeth went to work automatically and joyously. Sniffy McGurk crossed the path of a big French lumberjack, and he was knocked so deep into the hole for the flag pole that, he said, it took him two days to climb out.

The argument was still under way when he got back to the surface. The crews had wrecked the village, and most of the debaters were fighting miles away to the eastward on the shores of Bay de Noc. The name has real historical significance, for it means "bad knock."

This memorable meeting of Paul Bunyan's woods and loading crews was a mighty enjoyable affair, and a splendid time was
had by all. When the session adjourned because of total weariness
and the inability of the contestants to stand longer on two legs
or one leg, some of them didn't have clothes enough left to cover
the knee of a sparrow.

In due course the boys settled their differences without any
hard feelings, and planted and painted the big pole. On the
Fourth of July Paul Bunyan came over from Seney for a dedi-
cation service. There was an immense crowd, and Paul made a
rousing speech and raised an American flag with appropriate
ceremonies. The day was warm and delightful, the great throng
was responsive, and the iced punch on the speaker's platform
was spiked and authoritative.

Paul took a mighty pinch of snuff, and as he looked out over
the weaving mass, a grand idea came to him. Why not start a
pole-sitting contest? He allowed that it would be a fine thing
for the timber industry, and would help to keep the country
interested in the forests, and fire prevention, and conservation.

He took another swig of punch, shed his jumper, and climbed
the pole then and there, all ablaze with the vision of showing the
country the possibilities of an endurance test on a pole, with not
a limb to throw his leg over or a cross-piece on which to rest.

Within three days Paul's rivals and imitators were roosting
on telegraph and telephone poles, trees, lightning rods, silos, flag
poles and chimneys all over upper Michigan and northern Wisconsin. In less than a week folks in Key West, Labrador and
Alaska were competing for pole-sitting and tree-sitting prizes on
a mammoth scale.

Communities in every State and territory took up Paul's great
idea. So many messages and congratulations came to Hermansville that the boys rigged up a telephone line to Paul at the tip of
the pole, and relayed the good news from far and wide. Soon
people from Maine to Mexico were talking with Paul at his lofty
vantage point, and wishing him well and telling him what a genius
he was. He telephoned his gratification to the boys at the foot
of the pole, and said he could see that his pole-sitting idea had

been a real inspiration to millions and had thrilled the whole country.

While Paul was hugging the pole day after day away up there in the clouds, folks in Marquette and Ishpeming, one hundred miles away, couldn't understand why there was an eclipse of the sun every afternoon. Chickens in Munising and Negaunee went to roost three or four hours earlier than usual. A farmer near Michigamme dug his potatoes long before they were ripe and hustled them into his root house. He said he had a hunch that an early winter was coming.

Clothing stores in towns on the south shore of Lake Superior wired extra orders for Mackinaw coats, stag pants and jumpers to the Soo Woolen Mills in Sault Ste. Marie. And then, one fatal afternoon, when the grand champion pole-sitting prize of the United States and Canada was all but won, Paul went to sleep on the pole. It was a tall-pine, gosh-all-hemlock disaster.

He fell off the pole, turned twenty-seven flip-flops and forty-eight somersaults on the way down, as recorded by Truthful Tim, and lit away out in the center of Lake Superior. His left boot heel struck the Keweenaw Peninsula and broke off a big chunk of the mainland which fell fifty miles out in the lake not far from the Canadian shore.

The Canadians claimed this land as their own—they said Paul had kicked it over on their side of the international boundary, that no doubt it would stay there unless Paul moved it back, and therefore it rightfully belonged to them. But some of the biggest men in the country notified the Canadians that we would have the law on them if they dared to occupy the disputed territory. They held that the new island was American territory to begin with, and that it should remain so.

This explains the origin and the location of Isle Royale, the country's newest national park, and the most unique of all the parks. If Paul Bunyan had never had the idea of a pole-sitting contest there would be no Isle Royale national park today, and the boundary line wouldn't run north of the island and close to the Canadian shore.

But back to our big blue ox. One-Eye LaRue, the barn boss, never did forgive Babe for what happened the year Paul Bunyan and his crews logged the white pine stands of Dickinson county.

Paul was a great athlete. He liked to have his men go in for athletics and good clean sport in their spare time. He had a camp that year on the present site of Iron Mountain. One-Eye had organized a scrub baseball team of lumberjacks from Camp Ten, and he told the world he would risk his last dime on his team.

Johnny Inkslinger was captain that year of another team from Headquarters Camp Sixty-Nine. The boys smoothed off a baseball diamond in a clearing behind the sleeping camp, where One-Eye had been putting Babe out to grass. It was June and the days were long, and there was plenty of light for evening games. On the evening mentioned by Truthful Tim the boys had shooed Babe out of the lot, where he had been plucking grass and having a good rest.

It was the seventh inning and Johnny's team was in the field. Paul was umpire—the one umpire in all the world that no player ever talked back to. Johnny was pitching and One-Eye came to bat. One-Eye's sight wasn't the very best, but he waited for a pitch that suited him and batted out a long fly. From the side lines it looked like a sure home run.

One-Eye rounded first and second bases under full steam. The left fielder found the ball at the edge of the woods and heaved it to third with all his might. One-Eye saw the ball coming and he made a head first slide dive into what he thought was third base.

When he finally came up for air, plastered a rich, ripe brown, the lumberjacks laughed till they were weak, and Paul called for time out while he nearly threw a fit. Babe was away over near the woods and he laughed too, as much as an ox can laugh. A look at One-Eye was enough to make a horse laugh.

Paul said, "Shame on you, Babe," and he picked up One-Eye with a thumb and a finger very carefully by the seat of his pants, and told him to hunt up some more clothes. And for the rest of his life One-Eye was plagued over his accident at what he thought was third base.

When the boys wanted to stir up One-Eye after that, all they had to do was to ask him if he thought he could make third base. The question never failed to put him in the mood for murder, but when we remember Babe's size, who could blame One-Eye?

There never was a thriftier barn boss than One-Eye. He often loaned money to Paul Bunyan's French lumberjacks. Once a Frenchman borrowed a few dollars from him, and One-Eye insisted on security, or at least some evidence of the debt. This happened on a Sunday and the Frenchman sat for hours on his bunk with paper and pencil. He scratched his head, blinked, breathed hard, took innumerable pinches of snuff, and finally handed the following to One-Eye:

> For borrowed money I promise to pay
> T'ree four dollars in t'ree four day,
> And eef de money I don't bring,
> Why keep dis note, she's h'all same t'ing.

Tim is sure that One-Eye's folks still have the note.

Babe's health began to fail in the winter of logging operations in the hills north of Champion. When he refused to eat some juicy cat-tails, and when he wouldn't even sniff at a nice, fresh wriggling sucker caught for him by One-Eye in Safety Pin creek, the boys could see that Babe wasn't long for this world.

Few of the lumberjacks went to sleep that night. One-Eye sat up with Babe and gave him gallons of paregoric to ease his cramps. About four in the morning Babe gave a thunderous, heart-breaking moo and breathed his last. It was the end of the world's most famous ox of all time.

Paul Bunyan declared a half-holiday at camp, and the crew worked for hours digging Babe's grave behind the barn. "When I heard the clods rattling down on his poor old carcass, I just couldn't keep from crying," said Tim. "I was ashamed of myself for shedding tears over a gentleman cow; but Babe was a real gentleman after all, always honest and kind and willing, at least when he got all the cat-tails and suckers he wanted. And when I looked around I saw that all the other boys were crying, too.

"Then Paul burst out boo-hoo-hooing, and all hands simply broke down and spent the rest of the day weeping. We cried so hard that our tears flowed down into a ravine and formed the headwaters of the Escanaba river, which is still a good-sized stream. So that's how the Big Blue Ox was laid away, and may Heaven rest his poor old tired soul.

"A few days after Babe died, I read in a Detroit paper that a big crack had appeared in one of the city's tall buildings on the very night that Babe died. The echo of Babe's last moo must have cracked that wall," concluded Tim.

24

The Winter of the Black Snow

Paul Bunyan's walking boss for all camps was Forty Jones.

The walking boss in a Michigan northwoods camp corresponds to the personnel director in a big city establishment—he looks after the help and keeps the force up to requirements.

The boys called their walking boss "Forty" because he never hired or fired less than forty lumberjacks at one time. If logging was slack and a camp had twenty lumberjacks too many on the payroll, forty had to go, for that was Forty's mark. He said he hired 'em without notice and he fired 'em the same way.

Forty was a Cornishman, and he criticized Sourdough Sam's Norwegian style cooking. Forty loved Cornish pasties and had them sent to him from the Copper Country when Sam refused to cook them for him. Sam swore he never would demean himself by cooking pasties—he said they were invented by a baker in Cornwall who ended his criminal career in an insane asylum.

According to Sam, the baker who makes a Cornish pasty starts with a piece of dough the size of a flapjack and mixes it with beef suet—think of it, said Sam, beef suet, mind you! Then he rolls the dough flat, with its disgusting suet contents.

Next he piles potatoes, meat and onions on it, a cup of mustard and a pickle or two; some noodles, coffee essence, and a few beets; a cup of vinegar and a sprinkle of Florida water and maybe some gin, but think, said Sam of wasting good gin on a mess like that. Then he adds a dash of Worcestershire sauce, a pinch of cloves and two pinches of red pepper, and he douses the mass with cottonseed oil. Last, he folds the dough over the top of all this hash, like mother did with her apple turnovers. What a sacrilege, said Sam, what an abomination in the name of mother!

This done, Sam continued, the baker puts his Cornish turnover in the oven and bakes it till dark, and maybe all night and the next day. Then the Cornishman puts it in his pocket and forgets all about it until week after next, when he finds it and breaks his teeth on it. A swell dish, said Sam with a sneer full of sarcasm.

Sam added that the Cornish regiments in the British army made use of their pasties as gas bombs and cannonballs when they went into action. He said pasties were so called because the Cornish soldiers pasted their enemies in the eyes with them, and the execution was terrific. The boys guessed that maybe Sam and Forty didn't love one another as they should have done.

"I remember recklessly eating a Cornish pasty one night in Houghton," said Tim. "Twenty-five thousand pop-eyed devils held a convention on the foot of my bed from midnight until dawn. Another time I ate two pasties in one evening, and fifty-one thousand nine hundred and eighty fuzzy-faced, spike-tailed devils went to bed with me and played hide-and-go-seek for hours around and over my bunk.

"I've seen Forty Jones roll his eyes and swoon with delight as he surrounded one pasty after another. When we went to town with Forty and watched him eat saffron buns, Sniffy McGurk and I would debate sometimes whether Forty was a human being.

"But I started to tell you something about the Winter of the Black Snow. In order to understand how it happened, maybe you recall hearing of Awkward August, the camp gardener. Having a garden at every camp was an idea of Paul Bunyan's, and the gardens were fine investments as a rule. The most remarkable feature about August was his whiskers. They turned green every spring like Paul Bunyan's, only much more so.

"Scientists came all the way from Boston to investigate August's soup strainers," continued Tim. "When the buds were bursting and the grass was sprouting, August's alfalfa sprigs began to take on a greenish glint, and soon they blossomed out in full emerald tints. August called them his lace curtains, and said their annual change in hue proved that nature intended him to be a gardener.

"Yes, his lilacs were glorious, regular No. 10 EE width," said Tim. "They sure were an impressive demonstration of what a man can do by not letting his mind wander. August always insisted that they took on delicate bluish highlights when they began to alter with the changing season. But as he used them to wipe off the soil from his cabbage patch which accumulated on his hands, he could hardly be called an accurate judge of color.

"Late in July of each year these astounding chinchillas of August's took on a kind of hay complex, with a suggestion of going to seed, as it were. With one gradation after another his foliage was nearly white by the time the first snow fell. The lumberjacks couldn't explain it, and the phenomenon puzzled the scientists, beauticians, and upstate weather observers year after year.

"People who had gardens up and down the Seney road, and who had always relied on the moon's changes when planting carrots and radishes, watched the seasonal alterations in August's sassafras thicket and seeded accordingly. For years picnic dates in the Fox river country were set more and more each summer in line with the prevailing tint of August's bush at a given period.

"The lumberjacks agreed that August's spinach was almost human. In a high wind it flattened down on his chest as if to protect him from the blast. When it attained the emerald hue of spring, and threw out new shoots and dug into his collar bones, August knew that the time had come to climb out of his winter ganzies. By following his fernery around intelligently he avoided for many years the slightest sign of sore throat.

"More than once August was asked to sign up for research on his life's work at some scientific laboratory, but he said the Lake Superior country suited him and he hated the thought of leaving it. He said that after all, the northwoods were the place for him and he couldn't be happy anywhere else, even if the scientific sharps did offer him a big increase in pay for the privilege of studying his frontal entanglements.

"August's specialty was pumpkins. He said he wasn't no hell on onions or beggies, but that he could beat the world on pumpkins. He raised pumpkins so big that Sourdough Sam made more than five hundred pies from one pumpkin, and nearly half of it was left over.

"When we wanted to cross August's pumpkin patch that fall we had to dig a tunnel beneath the monsters. One of Paul's land-lookers strapped two of August's pumpkin seeds on his feet when he went snowshoeing the following winter. August toted one of the smaller pumpkins down to the State Fair in Escanaba and took five prizes with it, to say nothing of half a dozen grand champion ribbons, a free trip to Detroit and a nice letter from the Governor of Michigan.

"I remember that one year August planted forty acres of tobacco just across the fence from his cabbage plot. Millions of grasshoppers came and ate up most of the tobacco. Then the sassy things sat on the fence and spit tobacco juice all over the rows of cabbages.

"Paul Bunyan thought they would be a total loss, but Johnny Inkslinger told August to pull the cabbages as soon as they were ripe, dry them out and grind them up. They made an extra fine grade of bulk snoos, and we sold barrels of it from the van.

"August was a Hereford cattle fancier, too," continued Tim. "I recall the year when Paul cleared ten thousand acres of land near Round River and sowed it with grass seed. He and August went to the Chicago stockyards and bought five thousand Hereford yearlings. Paul shipped them to Round River and put them out to pasture with August in charge.

"Black bears were plentiful that year and they dragged off some of the yearlings. Paul decided to count his cattle, and he had an idea. The only bridge across the river was a hollow Norway pine. Paul drove the yearlings through the tree and counted them as they went in, and August counted them when they came out on the other side. August counted about two hundred less than Paul did, but when they walked through the tree they found the missing cattle in a hollow limb. August said it was a sizeable tree, but he had seen lots bigger ones in the old country.

"One spring Sourdough Sam wasn't feeling well. He asked August to plant a spinach patch—he said that spinach was rich in iron, and he allowed that he needed a tonic. August put his mind to work on the project, and he had an idea. He reckoned that still more iron in the spinach would do no harm. He asked Big Ole, the blacksmith, to break one of Babe's worn out logging chains into small pieces. August strewed the pieces over the garden patch and planted spinach seed where the iron was thickest.

"When the crop was ripe, Sam, thinking about the iron content, tested the spinach plants with a magnet. Sure enough, the spinach flew out of the ground and clung to the magnet in bunches. The very first plate of the ironized spinach put new life and pep into Sam. The same afternoon he hunted up his old enemy, Forty Jones, and knocked the daylights out of him.

"Paul Bunyan had a generous helping of the stuff for supper the same day. He climbed a tree before dark and hopped from branch to branch of a Norway pine one hundred feet above the ground. When he got back to earth he ordered Sam to put the woods crew on a straight diet of spinach until further notice. In the next three weeks the boys cut a pile of logs that would have done credit to a crew ten times the size.

"When they got tired of eating nothing but spinach August let the rest of the crop go to seed. Years later a mining geologist located an immense deposit of high grade iron ore on the spot, which is known today as the Lake Angeline pit in Ishpeming.

"No one can make us lumberjacks believe that iron doesn't grow in the ground, just like turnips or potatoes," said Tim. "If Awkward August didn't cause iron ore to grow there by letting his ironized spinach patch go to seed, then how in the world did the iron get there?

"Poor August came to a sorry end," continued Tim reflectively. "He was the awkwardest man on record, and it was a mistake to put him any place where there was a chance for trouble. August originally came to Paul Bunyan's camps as a woodsman, but he speared his leg with a peavy on his first day in the woods. When he got out and around he tripped over a root and broke his nose. Then he fell out of a tree when he was chasing a porcupine, and put his shoulder out of joint. Paul could see that August would never make a lumberjack, so August was put to work tending the camp garden, and there he made good.

"One winter we were logging at Hell Diver Lake, and we were short of men. Good lumberjacks were scare that winter in the Upper Peninsula, but Paul had an idea. He sent Forty Jones down to Mississippi, a lumbering State, where jacks might be plentiful.

"A couple of weeks later Forty came into camp with five

hundred colored lumberjacks from the long-leaf pine country. Paul put them to work dynamiting a hillside that was to be graded for a logging road. Every man who could be spared from camp was working on the hill, including Awkward August.

"One day when the colored lumberjacks were preparing to blast the rocks out of a stretch of new road, August was wandering in the vicinity when he stumbled over a fallen tree and dropped his pipe. The hot ashes fell on a fuse which the colored brothers from the sunny southland were attaching to a six-ton charge of dynamite, and touched it off.

"It snowed black the rest of the winter," said Tim solemnly, "and you can believe me or not, but the rains were colored until the following June. And that was the year when the end of August came in December."

25

Paul Goes Hunting

"Paul Bunyan was a great hunter. He loaded his shotgun with four dishpans of powder and a keg of spikes, and I've seen him shoot geese with it that were flying so high they spoiled before falling to the ground," said Truthful Tim.

"Paul could beat any Ojibway Indian when it came to tracking down game, and the Ojibways are the best hunters in the world. When Paul was on the track of an animal it didn't make a bit of difference to him whether it had rained or snowed the day before. Once when I was hunting with Paul we came upon the skeleton of a moose which had died of old age. Just to show me what he could do, Paul picked up the moose's trail and followed it back to the spot where the moose was born. I've never heard of an Indian who could do that.

"Paul was a famous partridge hunter, but he was never guilty of hunting partridges with a shot gun. He said it wasn't sportsmanlike. He used a rifle, and he shot the bird's head off. Strolling down a trail one morning Paul spied a bird forty rods away. All he could see was the head of a partridge on the other side of a log. Paul fired and the head disappeared, but rose almost immediately. He fired again and the head dropped, re-appearing a second later.

"He said this happened again and again. He was astonished at his poor marksmanship, but he kept on firing until he had thirty-one shots and ran out of bullets. When he investigated he found thirty-one partridges on the other side of the log, with their heads clipped off.

"During all the years I lived and worked in the upper Michigan forests I never saw a single wolf, and Paul said that he had never seen a wolf at large. Wolves are the most cowardly animals in the world; they are clever and cunning and they see you when you are in the bush, but you don't see them. Furthermore, wolves never attack human beings. If a man tells you that he has been et by a wolf, don't believe him.

"But in the old days there were many other strange and fearsome animals in the Upper Peninsula woods. Sometimes a hunter would bring a side-hill dodger into camp. The four legs on one side were six or eight inches shorter than the legs on the other side. The side-hill dodgers thus ran along the steep slopes of the hills as swiftly as a rabbit could travel on level ground.

"Paul Bunyan hunted down the last hodags before he was through logging off Michigan's Upper Peninsula. I have often seen their tracks on the rocks, and these tracks were usually five feet long and two feet wide, with claw-marks on all sides. Chris Crosshaul said that he had killed dozens of hodags, and he carried a hodag claw about eight inches long, which he used as a toothpick.

"Chris said that he usually trapped the hodags with a forty-pound meat-hook which he baited with a moose carcass and clamped to a tree trunk with a logging chain. According to Chris a full-grown hodag often weighed ten tons and was more than twenty feet in height, with two rows of bony spines on its back. Sometimes, Chris said, after the hodag had swallowed the hook, it bit through the four-inch steel chain and got away.

"Paul did a grand thing for the Upper Peninsula when he exterminated the pesky hodags. If the woods were filled with hodags today as they were many years ago, we can be sure that many deer hunters would find business so good at home that they never would be able to get away in the hunting season.

"There were times when the Lake Superior swamp dodgers gave us plenty of trouble. They sneaked into camp on dark and foggy nights and stole the lumberjacks' hair oil. They would patiently lie in wait for days just to get a taste of hair oil. Some folks called them hide-behinds, but their true name was swamp dodgers.

"These wily animals dodged from one swamp to another in search of their favorite food. Sometimes when we pursued them they would swallow themselves and thus evade capture. When Paul got tired of chasing the swamp dodgers he had Big Ole make dozens of swamp hooks, and with these we outsmarted the dodgers and hooked their legs together in deadfalls. Paul's invention is still in use for getting out pulpwood in Upper Peninsula camps.

"One night in the fall of '87, when Paul and I were returning to camp from a cruise in Mackinac county, we came upon the largest bear I ever seen. As it climbed head first down a tree, Paul grabbed it by the forelegs and I swung his big ax on its head. We toted the bear into camp—that is, Paul did—and had bear steaks for supper. Sourdough Sam fried out the fat and put down seven barrels of bear oil. Paul flavored the oil with cinnamon essence and smeared it on his whiskers when he went to call on Tiny. But the change from rose-scented vaseline was too much for Tiny, and she made him shave clean that winter.

"One-Eye LaRue had a remarkable experience with a bear, which shows how clever a bear can be. One morning, he said, he was walking to Thousand She-Devils Lake, when he saw clouds of bees flying out of a hole in the trunk of a big maple tree. He climbed the tree, threw his jumper over his head to keep the bees out of his eyes, and came down with more than twenty pounds of number one wild clover honey.

"He stowed the honey in his poke and started for camp, thinking how good the honey would taste on a stack of flapjacks in the morning. Then he heard a noise behind him, 'Woof! Woof!' He looked around and there was a big black bear. The bear was so blamed big, One-Eye said, that he must have weighed a ton and a half.

"Now every lumberjack knows that a bear will commit murder on sight if he can get enough honey. One-Eye said he could see that something would have to be done mighty quick. He didn't want to lose the honey, so he lost no time in climbing another tree. He was sure the bear would get tired of hanging around after a while and go away.

"He was partially right. After waiting about an hour under the tree for One-Eye to come down, the bear, tired of growling, sharpening his claws on the tree and drooling over the tree roots, started off toward Knockout Creek. One-Eye waited five minutes and began to climb down.

"When he was half way down the trunk, he said, he heard another 'Woof!' He made record time getting back up again to where he could straddle a limb. He told us that he simply couldn't believe his eyes when he looked down. 'You can dog my cats,' he said, 'if that bear hadn't gone over to the creek and brought back a big buck beaver. There was the bear, standing on his hind legs and beckoning to the beaver, just like he was saying: 'This way, friend, I have a job for you.'

" 'Yes,' said One Eye, 'and there was me, up a tree for fair, and cornered. The beaver waddled over to the tree where I was a-setting, and the bear came with him. They rubbed noses and whinnied, and I could see they were hatching trouble for me And then the bear, a-standing on his hind legs and looking to be all of eleven foot tall and not a blamed inch less,—the bear, I say, waved one fore paw at the beaver and the other at me up there in the tree, a-hanging on for dear life and wondering what was coming next. He was saying just as plain as words: 'Get ready, Beav, old pal, and do your stuff right here'—and with that the bear drew his fore paw across the foot of the tree.

" 'Boys, you can believe me or not,' said One-Eye, 'but as true as I'm a-telling you, the beaver looked at the bear with a gleam of understanding in his eye. He nodded his head, put his fore paws on the trunk, and began to bite chunks out of the tree big enough to keep a fire all night in a Quebec stove. And me up there on a limb with my eyes a-popping out so far that you could hang your hat on 'em.

" 'And mind you, there was the bear, a-waiting at the foot of the tree right behind the beaver, licking his chops and gnashing his teeth and drooling, all ready for me and the honey to fall into his outstretched arms. I heard a crack, and then another and a louder crack, and the tree started to fall toward the road. Just as it went over I gave an old-fashioned Indian yell and jumped for my life, and when I jumped, my poke fell plumb into the bear's up-reaching paws. I landed right side up and I bet you I made forty feet on the second jump. I'm a-telling you, boys, I didn't linger long around there. I made the two miles to camp in three minutes flat, a-yelling 'TIMBER!' all the way. And that cussed bear stole my honey after all, that I'd worked so hard for and climbed a tree to get!' "

"When I was at the Rag Bag Lake camp we went hunting

mice with rifles in our spare time. We called them Paul Bunyan mice, and they weighed up to eighty pounds apiece. These mice were the forerunners of the upper Michigan beavers, and they gave us considerable trouble the winter that Paul logged near the Daffodil River in Baraga County. I saw one of them walk off with a ten-pound pail of lard and a side of bacon.

"One day Big Ole and I were making a mouse trap in the blacksmith shop when a mouse came in and began to sharpen its teeth, which were four inches long, on the grindstone. Ole threw his hammer at the mouse and mashed its tail flat as it ran away. No one had ever seen a beaver in the Upper Peninsula woods up to that time. It's likely that the flat-tailed mouse became the ancestor of the beaver family. A beaver looks just like a big, furry mouse, and we lumberjacks have never doubted that the Upper Peninsula beavers are the result of the crossing of the flat-tailed mouse with the swamp muskrats.

"Some people have said that Paul was a great deer hunter, and that he invented deer hunting. The truth is that Paul never killed a deer. He said that one live deer is worth a thousand dead ones and that we ought to let the deer alone. He thought that the most beautiful and harmless thing in the bush is a little spotted fawn, and he said he never would be guilty of taking the life of something which did no harm and couldn't fight back.

"Many people like to think that Paul Bunyan was a blood-thirsty man and he liked nothing better than to see blood running. But he wouldn't even eat a piece of deer meat, for he said that a deer is usually frightened nearly to death before it is shot, and that fear fills its blood and tissues with poisons.

"One summer day Paul and I paddled from Munising over to the Pictured Rocks in his big canoe, for a day's timber cruise. We drew the canoe up on the shore and left it while we went into the bush. When we came down to the shore at evening the canoe had disappeared. We started to walk the shore back to camp when I saw the canoe away out on the bay. It was moving, but we couldn't see anyone in it.

"We climbed up on a high rock to get a better view, and you can believe me or not, as One-Eye says, but there were two tiny fawns, cuddled down in that canoe. And behind the canoe, with nothing but her nose showing above the surface of the water, was their mother, swimming, and pushing the canoe across the bay to Grand Island—taking a short cut away from danger. Paul and I walked into camp at midnight, and we agreed that the sight of the doe and her fawns in the canoe was well worth the trip. It wasn't in either one of us to feel sore at her for borrowing our canoe.

"Paul told me about a remarkable experiencee he had one time on the Deer Park Road. He was hunting for moose with an old musket, and he had no bullets left. He had taken a pocketful of dried cherries into the bush, and some of the pits were still in his pockets. He rammed down a dozen or so pits on the powder in his musket and let fly at a passing moose. He was sure he had hit the moose, but it got away.

"Some years later he was hunting in the vicinity, he said, when a mass of green timber began to move in his direction. The thing was so spooky that he felt like running for dear life, but he was a stout-hearted man, so he stood his ground, pulled himself together, aimed into the moving leafy mass and fired. Sure enough, the explanation of what had happened was very simple. He found a moose kicking and dying under the greenery, and it was the very animal he had wounded years before. The pits had taken root in the moose's hide and had covered the animal with a dozen living cherry trees.

"But I must tell you about the gillygaloo birds, great nuisances that lived around Gillygaloo Lake in Ontonagon County. Once when we were logging in that vicinity, a gillygaloo bird prowled around the camp for weeks, coming in nights and eating our ax handles. The bird was about twelve feet high, somewhat larger than an ostrich, and like all of its tribe it would go miles for a meal of ax handles. It loved ax handles like a bear loves honey, or a porcupine loves salt, or a swamp dodger loves hair oil.

"Paul told us lumberjacks that this bird must be captured, otherwise we would have to go out of business, for we were out of ax handles most of the time. So Big Ole dug out the inside of an ax handle and filled it with dynamite. Then he attached a fuse and laid in wait for the gillygaloo and caught it in the act.

"The bird swallowed the ax handle and was looking around

for more when Ole touched a lighted match to the fuse. The dynamite exploded in the gillygaloo's insides, and the bird made a noise like 'OOMP! OOMP!' and walked off. Ole couldn't understand until later why the gillygaloo didn't fly into pieces. Later on, Forty Jones caught the bird on the shore of Chief One-Sock lake, with a log chain snare.

"We found forty-seven ax handles in its stomach which, when spread out, measured yards each way and was tougher than red horse. Paul had it tanned and he roofed the van and the camp office with it. This happened nearly fifty years ago, and I understand that the gillygaloo's stomach is still keeping the rain off a shacker who moved in a year or two after Paul broke camp there.

"The Paul Bunyan Lumberjacks' Protective Association believes in keeping the former names of Upper Peninsula streams and lakes, when and wherever the names are fitting and proper. We are fighting the proposed move of certain people to change the name of Gillygaloo Lake to Gwendolyn Lake. There is something grandly historic about the word *Gillygaloo*. It has a pleasing sound and it makes visitors sit up and take notice. Why change it?

"And then these misguided persons are also trying to change the name of Rag Bag Creek on the maps to Fauntleroy Stream. There's no justice left in the world if this idea is adopted. They have offered to compromise with us and call it Tanglefoot Lake instead of Gillygaloo. That wouldn't be so bad, I think, not as bad as Gwendolyn, anyway. But Fauntleroy! Oh, mamma! Some folks have no sense at all of what is right and proper.

"There were many other strange birds in the oldtime Upper Peninsula—for example, the wiggletoe ducks that frequented Teal Lake in Marquette County. They had a way of bringing one toe to the nose and wiggling the others at us when flying high and out of range, and there was nothing we could do about it.

"Maple Syrup Lake is a few miles east of Pea Soup Lake in Delta County. Paul Bunyan made a hunting record at Maple Syrup Lake years ago that has never been beaten. He said he had been hunting for moose when he came out of the woods on the shore of this lake, with only one bullet left. Seven ducks were swimming on the lake, and straight across from him a bull moose was drinking, while he could see a big flock of geese right over-head. He said the spectacle of so much game made him dizzy, and while he was trying to look three ways at once he lost his balance and fell into the mud. When he got up he didn't notice that mud was clogging the barrel of his gun.

"With game everywhere, Paul said he just closed his eyes and pulled the trigger. The gun barrel burst and one piece of it sailed across the lake and killed the moose. Other pieces knocked the ducks over out on the lake and killed the geese overhead. The bullet killed a bobcat sitting on a high limb. Paul sat down suddenly when the gun kicked, and bagged four partridges that had been standing on a log behind him.

"With its dying jump the moose felled a big maple tree into the lake. The tree was so full of sap that the lake water was changed into maple syrup. For many years after that Cap Fisher, who was once a land looker for Paul Bunyan, served delicious maple syrup from the lake, with the famous flapjacks which he made in his Gladstone Hotel.

"While ducks were plentiful at Maple Syrup Lake, they were never as thick as I have seen them in the Thirty-Four Hills," said Tim. "I remember that when Sourdough Sam wanted duck for dinner, he simply pointed his rifle up the cook camp chimney and fired twice. Then he withdrew the rifle and placed a frying pan in position, and down would come two ducks into the pan. The birds were stripped of their feathers by the long fall. It's a pity, but those days have gone forever."

26

Lake Superior Wild Life

"The most ferocious, relentless and bloodthirsty American predator isn't the wolf, or the bear, or the bob-cat," said Tim. "It's the mosquito.

"In former years the Upper Peninsula mosquitos were the bane of our lives from May till September, until Paul Bunyan put a spell on them. He said the beggars had a right to enjoy themselves, but not all the year around. Paul put the Indian sign on them before he went away, and now they rarely bother anyone after the Fourth of July in this part of the country.

"In those days we had no screen doors or windows. The mosquitoes bored in and we took it standing up and lying down, in camp and in the bush. Maybe I should explain that the word 'bush' in this part of the country means more than just woods. Hardwoods, hemlocks, tamaracks, pines and pine plains, Norways, swamps and ridges were all bush to us. Of course the reader can hardly be blamed if he didn't quite understand this. Living in a big town, perhaps, as most readers do, and not having had the advantages of being a lumberjack, a tenderfoot could hardly be blamed for not being posted like we are.

"Today there probably isn't a mosquito in the Upper Peninsula of Michigan that measures more than four inches from wing tip to wing tip," continued Tim. "But in the old days at Soo Junction there were times when all hands had to stay in camp with the doors and windows barred. Outdoors, folks had to kick a hole in the swarms before they could spit.

"Every mosquito weighed two pounds or more and had a wing spread of up to fifteen inches. Sometimes we had to run from them to escape serious injury, while men armed with pike poles and pole axes fought off the pests. Fortunately for us, the big buck mosquitoes spent a good deal of time fighting each other over their lady friends.

"Paul Bunyan said he probably knew more about mosquitoes

than any other living man, having been brought up where they were the thickest. He told us that when he was a boy at his home down the Tahquamenon River, a swarm of mosquitoes chased him to shelter one day under his mother's soap kettle in the back yard. He said the mosquitoes attacked the kettle and sunk their stingers through the iron bottom. Paul clinched the stingers by kicking them with his heavy boots as fast as they came through, and the kettle flew away and was never heard of again.

"Paul had lots of confidence in himself—he said he was equal to anything—but his foot slipped the first time he tried to solve the mosquito problem. He sent to Texas for an extra large kind of bumble bee that he heard about, and he figured that they would grow and multiply and sting the mosquitoes to death. But the very day that Paul turned loose half a million of the big bees in the Tahquamenon swamp, they snuggled up to the mosquitoes and began to intermarry. Within thirty days they were bringing up families of half breeds that carried one stinger in front and another one behind, and they got us coming or going. In some places the swarms of skeeter-bees got so thick that we, too, had to kick holes in them before we could spit.

"One night four of us cookees were walking on the old Hendricks quarry tote road, when a pick ax whizzed past our ears. A mosquito had stolen it from the quarry section house and heaved it at us. Then a cloud of mosquitoes came down on us like murdering pirates, and kept us busy defending ourselves with clubs and rocks. After an hour's battle the swarm retreated into a nearby swamp, leaving their dead and wounded on the field, as well as a dozen pick axes.

"Darkness came on, and of a sudden the swamp seemed to be all afire. We couldn't believe our eyes when we saw the swarm returning with thousands of fire flies to light up the field of battle. That combination was too much for us, and we knew it was high time to get out of there, with a million mosquitoes advancing in mass formation and bringing a million fire flies to light the way. I picked up a dead mosquito and raced for the camp. Next morning I found that the mosquito carried a six-inch stinger.

"Another time I was walking on the Grand Marais road

when I saw a large bird at a distance, circling, then swooping down and apparently fighting something below. I ran across a field and hid behind a stump, and I found that two eagles were carrying on a combat with a giant mosquito. The eagles screamed and whirled and swooped together to their doom. The mosquito thrust its forward stinger into one of the birds and the rear stinger into the other, closed its legs on a sheep in the pasture, and flew northward toward the shore of Lake Superior. I took the dead eagles to camp and later Pete Vigeant mounted them in Sault Ste. Marie.

"Paul said that the mosquitoes were clearly our greatest predatory animal menace. I remember how they devoured a pair of Paul's mules one summer at the Sturgeon River camp. All we ever found of the mules was a harness buckle or two, and they were badly chewed. I saw one of the mosquitoes afterward, and he was picking his teeth with a wagon tongue and looking around for more mules.

"Before Paul put a charm on the mosquitoes they were very thick in the iron country of Upper Michigan, too. The Gogebic iron range mosquitoes were known by their iron-gray beaks which were stained by their drilling into the hills on all sides. At one time good diamond drillers were very scarce, and the mining companies established drilling schools for mosquitoes. The trained mosquito-prospectors drilled hundreds of nice, clean holes and discovered some of the biggest iron ore deposits on the great Gogebic range.

"The smoke smudge offered the best relief from mosquitoes in the early logging days, and when that didn't work we resorted to liquor. Paul Bunyan always drank the heaviest in May and June, when the mosquitoes were thickest. The lumberjacks had their little joke about Paul and the mosquitoes. They said he got so jingled in the evening that he didn't give a cuss for the mosquitoes; and then, along toward morning, the mosquitoes got so tight that they didn't give a cuss for Paul."

27

Big Ole, the Blacksmith

"Big Ole, the camp blacksmith, was mighty tall; not as tall as Paul was, of course, but Ole certainly was a big Swede," said Tim.

"Some people said that Ole was a prince or a count or something like that in Sweden years ago, and that he didn't care for a title and left his native land one night for America. The Swede lumberjacks looked up to Ole and some of them tacked his picture on the wall over their bunks. There's nothing as sentimental as a Swede, especially when he is eating hard tack or skorpors. A plate of hard tack certainly does bring up memories of home and mother if you are a Swede, but you have to be careful not to break a tooth when you're eating it," continued Tim.

"One time when Paul Bunyan was running a logging camp near Persimmons Lake, he broke the rim of his spectacles and one of his glasses dropped out. We were miles from an oculist and the accident was rather serious, as Paul had been writing some of his logging experiences for the papers, and he couldn't write without his glasses.

"Just then Ole walked into camp and asked for a blacksmith's job. The first thing he did was to solve Paul's trouble. He knocked the rim off an old bull-wheel, put it through the forge and welded it on to the frame of Paul's specs. That night Paul was writing for the papers again and Ole had a steady job with the promise of a raise if he kept on making good.

"Ole was one of the handiest men that ever punched a hole in a sinker. But then, we had to be handy to hold our jobs with Paul, for he just raised Cain when things went wrong. I remember the morning that Paul lost his pipe, there was no use trying to live with him that day. But when Ole found out about the loss, he fitted a piece of gas pipe into a coal oil barrel and made a dandy pipe for Paul. I never will forget the look of peace and contentment on Paul's face when he packed the new pipe

with Peerless and found that it was drawing well. I asked him for
a raise in pay then and there, and he granted it at once through
a cloud of smoke. I'm sure now that I could have had at least
five dollars more a month if I had been smart enough to ask
for it.

"One time when Paul was logging on Kidney Bean Creek,
which runs into Hot Potato River on the other side of Horse-
radish Hank's old skivver works, he had an idea that there ought
to be more music in the camp, that it would brighten things up
for us and make us better citizens. So he sent to Detroit for some
band instruments.

"The boys were slow in learning to play, and the horns were
too small for Paul, so he ordered Ole to hammer them all into
one big horn for him. One night before the job was done a flock
of hoot owls flew into the shop and made their nests in the instruments, unknown to Ole. When Ole got around to it he ham-
mered and welded them into one big horn which resembled a big
Dutch pipe, and thus the first saxophone was created.

"Paul mastered his big horn, and one foggy night he was playing it on the grounds of the Pivot Hotel, accompanied by the
band and the orchestra. The sound drifted out over Lake Superior, and seven lake captains made the mistake of thinking
they were listening to the Whitefish Point fog horn. They lost
their bearings in the fog and piled their ships up on the beach,
where the wrecks can still be seen near the Point. It was an un-
fortunate mistake, and the U.S. Coast Guard asked Paul to
kindly cut out his saxophone solos during foggy weather in the
future.

"The King of Sweden made Ole a present of a cornstalk
which has become famous. It was given to Ole, not to Paul
Bunyan as some people think. It grew with surprising swiftness
because it came within the influence of Paul's celebrated reversible clock.

"Originally the clock was just an ordinary affair, but Johnny
Inkslinger made an attachment for it that was little short of
wonderful. When Paul pushed the lever on the face of the clock
over to the right, all the trees and vegetables in the immediate
vicinity grew forty times faster than before. Paul could bring

timber to maturity in a few hours by using this clock. Any lumberjack can tell you how Paul lumbered the pyramid forty in the thirty-four hills three times in one day. He circulated around in the timber with the clock in his hand and a crew of loggers right behind him.

"Paul used the clock when he was logging on a scale basis, too. He could take a logging contract on the estimate of the owner's cruiser, and fairly double the estimated log output. The clock was as good as a gold mine to Paul, and it helped him to become a rich man.

"When he put the clock lever in reverse the surrounding trees, bushes and garden truck grew smaller instead of larger, and the sap stopped running in the trees. This gave Paul a splendid idea. He found that when he worked the lever back and forth in a clump of hard maples, the alternate movement of sap made a queer formation in the grain of the wood. This formation is called bird's eye maple and Paul Bunyan was its inventor. He worked the clock on only a few sections of hard maple at a time, and so he always controlled the market. When he went away he left some of these sections uncut, and they have made fortunes for the veneer manufacturing companies.

"And now to Ole's cornstalk," Tim went on. "When it came it was a tiny affair with roots buried in damp earth and wrapped in burlap. The day it came Ole was host to all the Swede lumberjacks at a party in the blacksmith shop. They toasted the King in schnapps, and the hardtack casualties were heavy. Finally they planted the cornstalk with formal ceremony in Awkward August's garden.

"After dinner Sourdough Sam noticed that the cook camp and kitchen were getting dark. He investigated and found that the cornstalk had grown to a height of fifty feet or so and that it was as big around as a pork barrel. When Paul arrived a few minutes later the stalk was twice as high and ten feet thick.

"Paul knew what the matter was. 'By the holy, old baldheaded Mackinaw,' he yelled, 'I'm a crooked-nose, peg-legged son of a camp cook if that reversible clock hasn't gone wrong again!' He ran for the clock, but it was missing. He ordered the cookees to find it and told Big Ole to climb up the stalk and cut off the top, thinking it could be killed that way.

"Ole had been kissing the baby and he was all ablaze over the progress his Swedish cornstalk was making. He said: 'Ven Ay vas yoost a kid in Sveden Ay used to play peaknuckle vid'—but Paul cut him short, 'Never mind the pinochle, Ole,' he yelled, 'up you go, before this blasted cornstalk of yours knocks the cook camp over.'

"So Ole started aloft, and in two minutes he was out of sight on the fast-growing stalk. We could hear him yelling, 'Hallup! Hallup!' and then his voice faded out. The commotion in the camp would have drowned the roar of a thunder storm.

"One-Eye LaRue was running rings around the cook camp like a wild man. Sourdough Sam slipped on a grease spot and knocked himself cold for nearly an hour. Elmer tried to bite the stalk, but it was growing so fast that it flipped him heels over head. Johnny Inkslinger ran out of the office and tried to figure the number of tons of corn sugar and syrup that could be realized from so lordly a stand of corn. A bobcat had chased a squirrel up the stalk and the cat soon fell, yowling and spitting. An ear of corn hit Awkward August on the head and put him out for the day.

"Paul was the only one who kept his senses. He grabbed an ax and tried to cut a chip out of the stalk, but every time he swung the ax, the hole moved up and closed. Then he took one end of a crosscut saw, with Chris Crosshaul and me on the other end, and we tried sawing, but we couldn't make a dent in the stalk. Paul thought he could hitch Babe to the stalk and pull it over, but we could see that it wouldn't do, for Babe would surely follow Ole up the stalk.

"Paul said there must be some way to head off the cussed thing from growing right up to the moon, and finally he had a grand idea. He hurried the woods crew over to the logging railway, and they tore up about a hundred rails and chained them all the way around the cornstalk. The stalk kept right on growing, and in the end it cut itself in two.

"Great was the fall of Ole's cornstalk. As for Ole, he had hung on somehow, somewhere near the top. The fall pitched him away over into the Mississippi river, and he never returned to the Upper Peninsula. He climbed out of the river and opened a blacksmith shop in Minneapolis, where he became the ancestor of I don't know how many Minnesota Swedes.

"When it was all over Babe hauled the remains of the cornstalk out of the garden, and Paul found his reversible clock behind the woodbox in the office, where Awkward August had knocked it when he went to the van for a package of flower seeds. The clock was running and the lever was away over to the right.

"I don't mean to say that Ole was the great-grandfather of all the Minnesota Swedes, but he must have helped a lot. In the following winter a Swede lumberjack came to camp when we were logging around Fuzzy Lake in Sciatica Township, Houghton County. His name was Aplis Johnson and we called him Peavy Face for short.

"Peavy was a good man with a landing crew, but Paul didn't like him because Peavy mixed skunk cabbage with his Peerless and thought it made a fine smoke. It smelled worse than a chunk of soft coal smouldering.

"One day Paul and Peavy were tugging together on Paul's canthook at a big pine log. They pulled so hard that the canthook handle was bent over like a bow. Just then, the wind being in the right direction, Paul inhaled a rank whiff from Peavy's pipe. It made him sick, and suddenly he relaxed his grip on the canthook handle.

"In a twinkling Peavy was soaring through the blue, headed west by southwest. Paul's nausea disappeared, and he smiled, yes, he laughed, as if he were saying: 'So you will try to gas me, will you?'

"What happened to Peavy Face Aplis Johnson? He sailed and sailed westward and landed in a Minnesota snowdrift. He dug himself out, got his bearings and thought he was in Sweden. That very day he wrote to his sweetheart Meenie in Oleolsonberg, Sweden. She crossed the ocean and settled down with Aplis, and due to the push given it by Meenie, Aplis, Big Ole, and a pretty little milk-fed Swede girl who thought Ole was a fine, tall pine, Minneapolis has become a large city. There must be half a million Swedes in Minneapolis today.

"Paul Bunyan told us one time that for one hundred years the French were the only white folks in the Upper Peninsula of Michigan. He said that they couldn't help losing out in the end because they had forgotten how to breed. He believed the north country was a natural home for the Swedes, because it is just like Sweden in climate, forests, scenery and so on, only more so.

"Paul warned me once not to feel bad if anyone called me a big Swede, which is slang for 'no good,' or it means 'quit your kidding,' or something like that. He said it was really a great honor and a compliment to be called a big Swede. So when I want to flatter some one, I call him a big Swede.

"Paul said that when a healthy, God-fearing young Swede couple were not afraid to get married on a small salary and to raise a big family, and when the children grew up to be number one Americans, decent and honest and a credit to their folks, it was a good thing for the country, and he for one said let 'em have the country and welcome, because they would never misuse it.

"Paul liked the Swedes. He said they made the best lumberjacks, and of course that meant the best citizens, because being a real lumberjack is the most important job in any country. Paul said the Swedes were going to run the country some day by sheer force of brains and babies, and he reckoned it would be a good thing if they did. He said that when it came to raising a family the rest of us couldn't compete.

"Some of the lumberjacks thought that Tiny was a Swede, and after supper, when the boys sat around the stove in the bunk camp, and told stories and sang lumberjack songs, there were lots of arguments about Paul and Tiny. Some thought that Tiny never should marry Paul and that she wasn't big enough for him. Others said that was all bosh,—that it didn't matter how small she was, she could marry Paul and sleep with him and maybe have twenty kids, and they would all be healthy and good American citizens.

"They said Paul was too modest, and that a strapping guy like him could father as many children as Big Ole or any other Swede could. There might be some doubt that Tiny could mother a great big family—but anyway, if they were in Tiny's place, they said, they wouldn't be afraid to take a chance with Paul Bunyan.

"That was only one of a thousand things we talked about around the sleeping camp fire in the long winter evenings. We sang 'Shanty Boy' and 'Bung Yer Eye' and many another good old swinging, roaring song. Sniffy McGurk was a good man with a fiddle and a real composer. He taught us a song about Paul and Tiny, that he said came to him like a flash one day when he was working with one of Paul's swamping crews over near Channing. We thought it was a grand song, but we were careful not to sing it when Paul was around.

"The first verse and the chorus went like this:

PAUL AND TINY

Paul Bunyan was the biggest man
    That ever walked the Earth;
He logged off northern Michigan
    For all that it was worth;
He logged the hills and hollers
    Of the Lake Superior land,
And he made a million dollars
    For to have at his command.

Chorus

And Paul had a gal, a pretty little gal,
    Tiny was her name,
    But he loved her just the same;
She was four foot one, he was seventeen foot,—
When they went to a dance he would take her in his boot;
    She stood on his toes
    And he waltzed her around,
    They would dance and prance,
    And she never touched the ground;
And everybody said—What a swell looking Nan
And her great big handsome brute of a man—
    But Paul danced on
    And he didn't give a damn,
For Paul, he loved his little Tiny gal,
And Tin-e-e she-e-e-e lo-o-oved Paul!

"There were about forty more verses by Sniffy, with a change in the chorus every third or fourth verse. I wish you could have heard us sing that song with maybe a thousand lumberjacks joining in the chorus. When they came to 'foot' and 'boot,' down crashed a thousand boots on the bunkhouse floor. And on the third from the last line in the chorus, all hands put lots of life into 'DAMN.'

"Sniffy's song about Paul and Tiny is famous, and you don't have to be a lumberjack or an Elk to sing it and enjoy it," said Tim. "We had a swell time, too, singing Chris Crosshaul's chantey about Lake Superior. Chris was a sailor on the Great Lakes before he reformed and became a bright light among the Paul Bunyan lumberjacks, and his song was called

SAILOR BILL

Bill was a tarry sailor man,
  As tough as a tar could be;
Built on the rolling, bowling plan,
  A salty old Will was Sailor Bill,
And he says to the mate, says he:
  "I've come for to sail on Superior,
Your mite of a tight little h'inland sea.

    Chorus: I've come for to sail on Superior,
           Your ca'm little, tight little h'inland sea.

"I've plowed the brine from Rome to the Rhine
  And back to the muddy Nile;
From Bantry Bay to old Cathay,
  A thousand thousand stormy mile;
And now I've come down to this 'ere," says he:
  "To sail on a bloomin' bucket of ile,
Your ca'm-like mite of an h'inland sea."

    To sail on a bloomin' bucket of ile,
      Your tight little tank of an h'inland sea.

So they sailed away from the Soo one day,
  On a balmy day in June;
And the lake was as still as an opium pill,
  And grievously sad was Sailor Bill
As he whistled a doleful tune;
  "Ho, for a gale and a rollin' sea!
I'm mighty sick o' this 'ere," says he.

    "Ho, for a gale and a rollin' sea;
     I'm mighty sick o' this 'ere," says he.

Then a gale came up on Superior,
  And down on the rocks they bore;
"It's an orful, turrible, 'orrible blow,
  A turrible, orful, 'orrible blow!"
Roared Bill as they hit the shore;
  And the wind it blew all his hair away,—
Cried he: "There's suttinly 'ell to pay!"

    And the wind it blew all his hair away,—
     Cried Bill: "There's suttinly 'ell to pay!"

Sailor Bill's unlucky bones
  Lie deep in the dark blue sea,
Down on the stones with Davy Jones;
  But his nightly ghost on the Whitefish coast
Goes wailing dismally,
  A-cursing his luck from keel to truck
And the ca'm-like mite of an h'inland sea!

    He's a-cursing his luck from keel to truck
     And the tight little, still little h'inland sea!

"Nobody could sing 'Shanty Boy' like Sniffy McGurk,"
continued Tim. "I've enjoyed it dozens of times. It goes like
this:

SHANTY BOY

I am a jolly shanty boy
    Who loves to sing and dance;
I wonder what my girl would say
    If she could see my pants.

With fourteen patches on the knees
    And six upon the stern;
I'll wear them while I'm in the woods
    And home when I return.

For I am on my jolly way,
    I spend my money free;
I've got plenty, come and drink
    A lager beer with me.

I'll write my love a letter,
    I'll give the ink a tip,
And if that don't bring her up to time
    I guess I'll let her slip.

Those dark-eyed single lassies,
    They think a heap of me,
You ought to see me throw myself
    When I go on a spree.

Now to conclude and finish,
    I hope I've offended none;
I've told you of my troubles
    Since the day that I begun.

With patched-up clothes and rubber boots
    And mud up to my knees,
I am a jolly shanty boy,
    A-fighting with the fleas.

"Then it was lots of fun to hear Bill Half-a-day, fine, hand-some, burly Ojibway, chant his Indian Love Song. We helped him chant it—that is, when he gave the signal, we all came down heavy on the 'Ugh!' Here it is:

INDIAN LOVE SONG

Nice night
    In June,
Stars shine,
    Big moon;
Walk on shore,
    Pretty little squaw,
Then we clinch,
    Haw!
    UGH!

Me say,
    Me love,
She coo
    Like dove;
Me smart,
    Me fast,
Big Injun, me,
    Never let chance pass;
Get hitched?
    Me say;
Uh, huh,
    She say,
    UGH!

Wedding bells
    Soon ring,
Honeymoon,
    Everyt'ing;
Happy now,
    Got pretty little squaw;
Settle down,
    Haw!
    UGH!

'Nother night
  In June,
Stars shine,
  Big moon;
Ain't happy
  No more,
Twins they cry,
  Walk floor,
  UGH!

Squaw mad,
  Her fuss;
Me mad, too,
  Me cuss,
  UGH!

Squaw she howl,
  Pappooses they yowl,
  Haw!
Sure, me big Injun,
  Me smart,
  Me fast,
But me know now,
  At last,
Me too damn fast,
  And how!
  UGH!

"Sniffy had another song that the boys liked,

BUNG YER EYE

I love a girl in Manistique,
　　She lives with her mother.
I defy all Michigan
　　To find such another.
She's tall and slim, her hair is red,
　　Her face is plump and pretty;
She's my daisy, Sunday, best-day girl,
　　And her front name is Kitty.

(CHORUS)

Bung yer eye! Bung yer eye!
　　She's wise and kind and witty;
She's my daisy, Sunday, best-day girl,
　　And her front name is Kitty.

I took her to a dance one night,
　　A sailor did the bidding;
Paul Bunyan bossed the whole shebang,
　　While Big Dan kept on fiddling.
We danced and sang the livelong night,
　　With fights between the dancing,
Till Paul cleaned out the whole damned place
　　And sent the sailors prancing.

Bung yer eye! Bung yer eye!
　　Oh, listen to my ditty;
She's my week-day, Sunday, all-day girl,
　　Oh, what a pearl is Kitty!

"There was still another song that we were fond of," continued Tim, "about the Sturgeon River. There are two or three Sturgeon Rivers in the Upper Peninsula, and Johnny Styles could have met his death on any of them. It was called

THE OLD TAMARACK DAM

Come, all you brave boys of the river,
    And listen to me for awhile;
I'll tell you the thing that befell him,
    My friend and my chum, Johnny Styles.

We were camped on the wild Sturgeon River
    Just below the old Tamarack Dam;
When we rose from our blankets one morning
    We saw on the rocks a big jam.

As soon as we'd eaten our breakfast
    We struck for the head of the jam,
And two of our boys took the pole trail
    To open the reservoir dam.

We worked for an hour and a quarter
    Up-hauling, but all in despair,
When finally the water worked through her,
    And like lightning she pulled out of there.

We rode her down to dead water,
    Our foreman cried, "Boys, all obey;"
Not a man in that crew but could ride her;
    Not a man in that crew was afraid.

On timber there was none any better
    Than my friend and my chum, Johnny Styles;
He rode her more often than any,
    For he always was reckless and wild.

But this day his luck turned against him,
    For he got his foot caught in the jam;
But he never once squealed till 'twas over,
    For Johnny had plenty of sand.

We rode her down to the dead water
  And worked till the sweat down did pour;
We pulled his cold corpse from in under,
  But it looked like poor Johnny no more.

Every bone in his body was broken,
  And his flesh hung in tatters and strings.
We buried him down by the river,
  Where the lark and the whippoorwill sings.

Oh, it's down by the wild Sturgeon River
  Poor Johnny lies under the sod;
On earth we found rest for his body,
  And we hope that his spirit's with God.

"We generally wound up the evening with 'Ole Pete Bateese'," said Tim. "We all knew the words and we went along with One-Eye LaRue leading. One-Eye had a good tenor voice and a sense of drama. Here it is:

OLE PETE BATEESE

Ole Pete Bateese got chase one nught
    By wolf up by de Soo;
Dese wolf dey t'ree, four in de pack
    And dey scare him tru and tru.

Pretty soon ole Pete climb up a tree,
    He t'ink he stay awhile;
Dese wolf dey sit down in de snow
    And lick dere chops and smile.

Pretty quick two wolf go trot away;
    Pete t'ink de rest soon go.
Pretty quick does wolf come right straight back;
    Pete's spirits dey sink low.

For w't you t'ink dese wolf dey got?
    Big beavers—one? No—two!
Dey set dem down beside dat tree
    And say, "By gar, now chew."

Dose beavers start in chew dat tree,
    Dey chew like beat de band;
Pete t'ink he soon be on de groun'
    Unless he take a hand.

So Pete pull out his one-quart hooch
    And let it run out slow;
It trickle down de trunk to where
    Dose beaver chew below.

Dose beaver, dey got drunk, by gar,
    Dey don't see none too good.
Dey mak mistake and chew de wolf
    Instead of chew de wood.

Dose wolf run 'way, and Pete climb down
    And sit down in de snow,
And cry and cry to t'ink for where
    His one-quart hooch she go.

"The last thing before turning in, we sang another verse or two of 'Paul and Tiny,' and we closed with the final chorus in honor of Paul Bunyan,

> He didn't give a damn for any damn man
> That didn't give a damn for him!

"Then we went to our bunks happy and cheerful and all set for a good night's rest.

"I can hear the boys right now, singing that grand old song about Paul and his pretty little Finn girl," concluded Tim. "Of course, you can readily understand why we didn't cut loose on it when Paul was around.

"Ah, but them were the happy days! Oh, boy, if they could only come again!"

28

Joe Kadunk's Blueberry Pie

"But I must tell you about one of the greatest inventions of modern times, made here in the north country," continued Truthful Tim.

"I was a cookee for Sourdough Sam at the Fishdam River camp in the hot summer of '84. "I never will forget that summer. The weather was so hot that I dug baked potatoes out of the camp garden in August. We plucked and ate roasted ears of green corn right off the stalk that year.

"It was then we lost One-Eye LaRue. Poor old One-Eye was out with the boys one night and later he fell into a bin of Babe's cat-tail fodder. All there was left of him was a metal clasp on his galluses.

"We cookees ran great risks when we went to the garden for cabbages. Chris Crosshaul started to walk across the cabbage patch one day without his gas mask. It took three hours for us to bring him around.

"This mishap gave Paul Bunyan an idea. He ordered a shipment of corned beef and sowed it among the cabbage heads. Some weeks later we harvested a wonderful crop of corned beef and cabbage. It averaged more than nine tons to the acre.

"That gave Johnny an idea. He organized the U.P. Corned Beef and Cabbage Improvement Association, and printed details of the experiment in a 300-page book, "Save Money By Growing Your Own Corned Beef and Cabbage."

"We lost Alexander, our tomcat ex-champion, that summer. He was prowling through the popcorn section of the camp garden when the hot weather began to pop the corn. Poor Aleck saw it, thought it was snow, and froze to death.

"We cookees cut and stored the rest of the cabbage crop in the camp root house, being mighty careful to keep our gas masks handy. Sourdough Sam salted down more than half of the cabbage, and before long he was piping hundreds of gallons of sauer kraut juice daily out of the root house. He said it was the finest thing in the world for the complexion and the general health. Every Saturday night he filled a wash tub with sauer kraut juice and took what he called a schlitz bath in it before paying a Sunday visit to his girl over at Gwinn.

"It was really warm that summer. Lucy, the camp cow, gave down boiled milk every day for weeks. I remember how a terrific racket routed us out of bed at five o'clock one Sunday morning. We found that the heat had turned Babe's horns into fire sirens. Babe had such a bad scare that he was cross-eyed the rest of the summer.

"We kept a flock of chickens at the camp that year—Poland Chinas, I think Sourdough Sam said they were—and the ground was so baked and dry that sparks flew when the chickens scratched gravel. The only way we could gather the eggs before they were hard boiled was to put a cake of ice in every nest. Sourdough Sam was dumping ice in a nest one day when the ice turned to boiling water and scalded his hands.

"The traveling parson told us once that some good always comes out of evil, and out of the hot summer of '84 there came Joe Kadunk's grand invention of blueberry pie. Joe was our second cook, and sometimes when a camp wasn't too large he did all the cooking. No one ever thought of making a pie with blueberries until Joe had his great inspiration. Folks ate the fresh picked berries, or they made blueberry sauce or blueberry wine. In those days, of course, the blueberries were too big for a pie of ordinary size. Not a berry of the '84 crop was smaller than a goose egg.

"Joe Kadunk was cooking at the Fishdam camp while Sourdough Sam was busy over at Pea Soup Lake. On the morning of August 26 Joe said to us at breakfast: 'Boys, things are slack in camp just now, and Mr. Bunyan has sent word that if you would like to pick blueberries today and tomorrow and maybe next day, you can go out in the bush and welcome, and your time won't be docked. Now, if you'll just bring in a good supply of blueberries I'll have a pleasant surprise for you day after tomorrow. That's my birthday and I'm going to throw a party for you.'

" 'Sure we'll pick the berries while you're getting the rest of the birthday dinner ready,' we told him. But we couldn't see how he could possibly make any blueberry wine by that time, at least wine with any authority. We mentioned that to Joe.

" 'Never mind, boys,' said Joe. 'I've got a splendid idea. You bring in the berries and I'll do the rest. Bring lots and lots of 'em.'

"So we went out on the blueberry plains and picked forty thousand quarts of berries and toted them in to the cook camp. Next day we brought in as many more. Bright and early on Joe's birthday, he asked us to haul the big concrete mixer over to the edge of a hollow that was once a small lake bed.

"Sniffy McGurk and some of the boys couldn't understand at first what it was all about, but I began to glimpse the big idea and the wonderful thought of Joe Kadunk. The hollow was shaped like a big pie tin, just right for the world's first, biggest and best blueberry pie.

"We spotted the mixer, and Joe explained: 'Boys, I've figured out that I can make a whale of a birthday pie with these blueberries, right here in this hollow. This is a historic occasion. We're going to make a whopper of a pie on this hallowed spot; a pie, mind you, made of blueberries, the first one on record and the biggest and most original pie ever made. This here spot will be famous for all time to come, for you're not only going to help me make this wonderful pie, but you're going to help me eat it, too, right here, see!'

"Yes, we saw without a bit of trouble what a grand thing the event would be for all of us. We could see that such a pie would make Joe Kadunk and the Paul Bunyan logging camps more famous than ever. It would be something to remember with a thrill for years to come. How sorry I am that we didn't take a picture of Joe's birthday pie!

"We were a busy crowd that day. First we up-ended and poured seven hundred barrels of flour into the mixer, and added water. Soon the dough flowed like a waterfall into that natural pie tin which once was Flannigan's Lake, and is known today and for all time to come as Blueberry Pie Hollow.

"Then Joe ordered the crew to take off their boots and socks and get out there on the old lake bed and its covering of sweet-smelling dough. We tramped around on the dough-sheet and smoothed it down carefully, making it ready for the berries. You understand we washed our feet first, of course. Joe insisted on the foot-washing. He said he wasn't taking any chances of spoiling the flavor and maybe making a Molly Hogan of his first big blueberry pie.

"When the dough was nicely spread on the hollow's bottom and sides, we sluiced our tons and tons of berries over it, using the old log-slide on the slope of Kill-Devil hill. Then we leveled off the berries and spread a dough blanket over them that was just right for baking into a nice, crispy crust.

"The weather was hot in the morning, about 110 degrees in the shade, and it kept getting hotter. Joe had a special report from the Escanaba weather bureau, 'very hot in the afternoon,' and sure enough the mercury rose to 263 degrees, and no shade. By three o'clock the heat was unusual, and by five o'clock the pie was done to a turn and the air was cooler.

"Precisely at supper time—six o'clock—Joe Kadunk lined us up around the pie. He tried it with a peavy and pronounced it well and truly done.

" 'Get ready!' he yelled. 'All ready!' We were up on our toes. 'GO!' and his pistol cracked.

"We went. I never saw such a rush, but then, I never have seen another pie like that, either. Bill Half-a-day was one jump ahead of me, and he made a high dive and shot into the pie head first. I was right behind him and his bare heel nicked my forehead.

"We wallowed up to our ears in that heavenly blueberry pie for thirty-six hours of bliss. No one ever had dreamed before how delicious a blueberry pie could be, and how much better the berries taste when they are baked in a pie.

"There we stayed, all cares forgot, right in the middle of the most magnificent pie ever conceived by a genius before or since. We ate and ate until we were full up to the ears.

"On the second night of the pie, Babe broke out of his stall. When the sun rose there stood the Big Blue Ox, mired, happy and contented, in the center of what was left of Joe Kadunk's inspired conception. That morning Babe must have weighed half a ton more than usual, and he was cracking a foolish cross-eyed smile from ear to ear. We tried to coax him out with armfuls of cat-tails, but he refused to leave the pie until dark. For months afterward he was bluer than ever.

"This was the real beginning of the great blueberry pie industry. It was founded by Joe Kadunk, second cook for Paul Bunyan, on his twenty-ninth birthday, August 27, 1884, at Blueberry Pie Hollow near the Fishdam River in Delta County, Upper Peninsula of Michigan. The industry was practically the only one in the country that made money during the great depression after 1929, and it keeps right on growing.

"Johnny Inkslinger ran the road roller across the remnants of Joe Kadunk's pie in the hollow, and saved fourteen barrels of blue ink for use in the camp office. Two days later a tramp lumberjack came into camp and asked for blueberry pie. We shot him at sunrise.

"Before long a few Upper Peninsula housewives tried out Joe's great idea, on a small scale, of course, and they began to make blueberry pies for their family tables. Then folks from many other places, visitors who came to the Lake Superior region in summer, discovered the surpassing goodness of blueberry pie. They have been eating all they could get of it since, and have been calling for more.

"I suppose no one ever did have enough blueberry pie, unless it was us lumberjacks, and of course there's never been another pie like Joe Kadunk's since," said Tim. "Honest, now, did you ever hear of anybody's refusing a second piece of blueberry pie, or an eighth, if there was any left?

"Not long ago a New York man mailed thousands of questionnaires into every State, asking people to name their favorite food. A couple of thousand Upper Peninsula folks answered, and all but two voted for blueberry pie. The other two preferred fresh blueberries with cream and sugar.

"Paul Bunyan told us afterward how sorry he was to miss

Joe Kadunk's blueberry pie birthday celebration. He was in Gladstone that day, when he invented the noble art of birling and started the first Gladstone Rodeo on its way.

"Maybe you don't know," Tim added, "that a birler is a man or a woman who can ride a whirling log in rough or quiet water. They say that Paul Bunyan spun a log so fast in Gladstone harbor that day, that the bark slipped off the log and he walked ashore on the bubbles. There's real birling for you. Later he taught some of us how to birl, and our children and grandchildren are doing many birling stunts at the Gladstone Rodeo each summer in peace times.

"Paul ordered that henceforth August 27 was to be celebrated annually in all of his camps as Blueberry Pie Day. People everywhere followed suit and began to eat blueberry pie.

"Thus," concluded Truthful Tim, "primarily through the logging operations of Paul Bunyan, and the inventive genius of Joe Kadunk, the bounteous blessing of blueberry pie has encircled the Earth and brought joy to many hearts."

29

Paul Goes Away

"It's a grievous matter to me and my fellow lumberjacks to even think of Paul Bunyan's passing," said Truthful Tim. "But the world is entitled to know the facts, so here goes.

"Every one of us cookees and lumberjacks were sure that Paul Bunyan would go right on logging pine and hemlock and hardwood forever. We couldn't imagine Paul's dying, or leaving the Lake Superior country. But many of us did outlive him, or at least we remained in the world longer than he did.

"There are reports that Paul died the death of a hero," continued Tim. "I know about them, and so do my lumberjack friends, but we never think of him as being really dead. For Paul Bunyan was no ordinary man. We don't pay any attention to the gossip about his dying with a broken heart after Tiny jilted him, either.

"True, she was the prettiest little pink-and-white China doll you ever saw, and the fact that she was once Paul's lady friend has made her Michigan's most famous woman. And when you stop to think of it, that's fame enough for any woman,—to have been known and liked and squired by Paul Bunyan, to have had her picture on his camp desk, and to be forever a legend in the Lake Superior region.

"Now, as for me—well, I can't even tell you Tiny's last name. That's all I care about women, and I think Paul Bunyan was much the same. He was too busy getting out timber products for the housing and the comfort of the growing midwest to pay much attention to any dame. When Tiny flouted him and went off with Con Kilhane, Paul must have felt that fate had done him a good turn and that it had been a close call. He knew he was lucky, or thought he was, anyway, and so did we.

"The way Paul passed on, or out, or up, was the most marvelous thing about a marvelous career. I had a foreboding, a slight one, that something was going to happen when he quit chewing Peerless, and when I heard that he no longer practiced evenings on the saxophone and the big bull fiddle. Maybe he had what they call a premonition, but if so, he gave no sign.

"I have the story from Steve Lowney himself, the world's best timber cruiser and a truthful man if there ever was one. Paul and Steve were looking over a tract of pine near Miner's Castle, at the Pictured Rocks. Paul was figuring on a logging contract with a Munising concern. The lumber market was firm and the big sawmill at Munising was running day and night.

"Paul and Steve had been inland that morning, and about noon they came out on the shore of Lake Superior, on the high plateau of the Pictured Rocks. It was near the spot where Paul once had a remarkable experience.

"Once upon a time one of Paul's crews was cutting timber on those same highlands. They rolled the logs off a 200-foot precipice, and Paul stood on the beach at the foot of the cliffs with his canthook in hand, catching the logs as they were thrown over to him.

"Over came a big maple log measuring probably a couple of thousand board feet. Paul saw it coming, but just then his foot slipped a little. Down fell the log on him, driving him into the sand and the underlying rock almost to his hips. He was a little lame for the next week or two.

"Steve said that on Paul's last day in the world, the great logger looked out over the lake for a long time. Then he stretched out flat and peered over the edge of the cliff. Steve could never figure out whether Paul was looking for the place on the beach where his legs had been driven into the rock, or whether he was inspecting some of the pictures he had drawn on the rocks in years gone by.

"A young maple tree was growing out of a crack in the rock about three feet below him. Paul reached over and grasped it, then he edged down further. The tree broke suddenly and Paul went over the edge.

"He was wearing a pair of high-top boots that day, with rubber soles perhaps a foot thick, and with rubber heels about as thick as three butts of eating tobacco. Steve was the only witness, and he was sure that Paul would be killed by the fall to the beach two hundred feet below.

"But Paul had turned once or twice in the air and landed right side up, and Steve said that he bounced at least a mile high. He fell from that great height, struck the beach standing up, and bounced about three miles high. And then, Steve said, Paul kept right on bouncing and whizzing past the top of the cliff, like a giant skyrocket. I never could have believed it if anyone else but Steve had told me how Paul bounced and whizzed.

"In less than ten minutes Paul was bouncing ten miles or more. Once he came down on Miner's Castle and knocked a corner off it. The very next time he came down he wrecked the Grand Portal, and no ship will ever sail beneath that gigantic arch again. It was a terrible situation. There was Paul, going up and coming down, coming down and going up, and not a blamed thing could be done to stop him or even slow him down.

"The camp wasn't far away, and Steve ran over and called to Sourdough Sam and Chris Crosshaul to drop everything and come quick. When they ran to the edge of the cliffs and saw Paul bouncing and whizzing, and trying to tell them something when he flew past, they were so unnerved, Steve related, that all they could do was to sit on the edge and let their feet hang over while they cried and cried, and Steve cried with them.

"By and by Sam pulled himself together and ran back to camp for a portable stove. He fried a pan of sinkers and Chris did his best to punch holes in them like Big Ole's. They knew Paul must be hungry, and they threw the sinkers out toward him as he went up and came down, in the hope that they might keep him from starving to death. But Paul bounced so hard and so fast that they couldn't reach him, and every time he went up he went higher and stayed up longer.

"Steve and Sam, Chris and Johnny and the others were like men in a nightmare. They wrung their hands and wept hysterically, and waited for Paul to stop bouncing. But he kept right on bouncing and finally he disappeared.

"When he came down the last time he dropped a scrawled note to the boys, bidding them goodbye and wishing them good luck, and saying he was hungry and almost shaken to pieces.

"He wrote that he had just bounced past the planet Venus and had seen some likely-looking timber there. He allowed that if he had good luck he would land on Venus when he went up again. Meanwhile, he said, he hoped we'd get along well with one another, and that we mustn't get tight too often, but that we should follow his example, always speak the truth, and live so that we could look any damn man square in the eye and tell him to go to hell. No crew of lumberjacks anywhere ever got better advice than that.

"So Paul Bunyan wasn't killed by shooting, as some folks say, and he didn't move to Alaska. He died with his boots on—that is, if he's really dead, which I doubt very much—and he bounced out of the world in a most remarkable way.

"We lumberjacks are sure that Paul is logging the pines on the planet Venus this very day. Probably they needed him on Venus, and he took a wonderful way to get there, I think. Steve Lowney thinks the same as I do."

30

He'll Be Back Some Day

"One day last summer Pete Vigeant and I were trolling in Lake Superior near the Pictured Rocks," said Truthful Tim, "when I hauled in a 70-pound Mackinaw trout.

" 'Just like old times,' Pete said to me. 'It reminds me of the days when Paul Bunyan was with us.'

"It was a sorrowful crowd of lumberjacks that Paul left behind when he started on his great trek. Most of us had worked for Paul a long time. We had played rummy with him, gone hunting and fishing with him, borrowed his eating tobacco lots of times. He treated us like men should be treated, except maybe now and then when he was away behind schedule on some logging contract. No, we'll never forget Paul Bunyan.

"I was dipping snoos and thinking hard for quite a while between bites. I said to Pete: 'Maybe Paul will come back some time.'

" 'What makes you think that?' Pete asked. He was trimming a bucktail fly with Paul's penknife. He always carries it with him when he goes fishing, and it always makes me think of Paul.

"And then I explained to Pete that Paul Bunyan didn't die as ordinary men do. We don't know for sure that Paul is dead or alive. He bounced out of the world, and there's no reason I know of why he couldn't bounce back, if he is still alive.

"Suppose now, that Paul is alive. If he should drop back here and come down in Lake Superior, for instance, he could fish himself out, couldn't he? Or if he came down on the Grand Marais sand dunes, we'll say, and slid into the lake, he could easily swim ashore, for he was a powerful swimmer. Did I ever tell you about the time he swam all the way around Lake Superior, then down St. Mary's river and around Lake Huron and Lake Michigan and back? It's a mighty interesting story.

"If Paul could come back today, he'd be glad to help us rebuild the forests. He knew more about trees than any other man who ever lived. He was criticized, of course, for cutting down thousands of acres of northland timber and leaving a lot of pine barrels behind, but he once said to me:

" 'Tim, after I'm gone folks here and there may complain that I despoiled the woods, but that doesn't worry me. I reckon the great Mississippi valley never could have developed as it did, if I and my crews hadn't stuck to the job of supplying the timber now housing millions of Americans in the central west.

" 'I'm doing my bit to make America great and useful. There hasn't been time to plant where we reaped, but there will be other timber crops in the years to come, if people are careful to keep fire out of the woods.

" 'We timbermen are passing along the life of the trees into the lives of the people,' said Paul. 'Timber was made to be used, and I am helping others to put it to good use. Trees grow old just as humans do and they should be logged and used in their prime, not when they are sapless and their hearts are gone.

" 'My big regret is that we couldn't plant two trees every time we chopped one down. But you've never heard of my being careless with fire in the woods, or of leaving a campfire until I was sure it was out.

" 'Another thing, Tim,' said Paul, 'I'm working out plans for what I call selective logging. That means cutting only mature or over-mature timber, and leaving the rest to grow up to maturity and reseed the ground and be cut later. When we learn how to do that effectively, the woods will soar aloft forever green and lovely; provided always, Tim, that fire is kept out of the forests. I've had the idea in mind for years, and if I'm spared I'll do my best to work it out.'

"Well, Paul had to go before he could put a selective logging plan into effect. He cut a lot of timber, but there is plenty left and there will be a great deal more. Paul's disciples are planting trees everywhere in the national and state forests. Best of all, they are scotching forest fires almost before they start. Their motto is the same as Paul Bunyan's: Use timber in the right way, and don't burn it up.

"Today's foresters and lumbermen would be the first to tell you that they cannot carry on a logging job as efficiently as Paul

Bunyan did—Paul having been the inventor of logging and the greatest logger of them all. Nevertheless they are bringing all-round selective logging nearer, and they want to keep the Upper Peninsula of Michigan as green and beautiful forever as it is today. And of course they are doing their level best to keep fire out of the woods.

"We lumberjacks are sure that Paul will come back, maybe in a year or two. There's a powerful lot of logging to be done here yet, and no one can possibly do it like Paul Bunyan could. But if we burn up our woods we'll never see him here again, for there would be nothing for him to do if he did come back. He could plant, of course, but he was always a man who liked to reap, too.

"All of Paul's lumberjacks who are still alive make it a point to keep their dues paid, if possible, in the Paul Bunyan Lumberjacks' Protective Association. We figure that Paul is alive and well somewhere, and that he surely will come back to Upper Michigan. Steve Lowney says he wouldn't be a bit surprised if Paul happened along any day for a woods cruise. That faith of Steve's is mighty fine.

"Our association holds regular meetings and we feel that Paul's absence is only temporary. He is our honorary president emeritus. Some of us boys have a little difficulty with the title, but everybody knows that our hearts are right, and that our great profession has done wonders under the leadership of a man who was an ornament and a glory to his country.

"When our secretary reads the roll at our meetings, Paul Bunyan's name is always called. We never doubt that some night on the second Tuesday of the month, he will walk in and answer, 'HERE!'

"So I'm telling you, friends, and warning you, that if you hope to run across Paul Bunyan some time in the Upper Peninsula woods, logging away at the job he loved so well, you must keep in mind what he told us over and over again, and be careful with fire in the woods.

"If we can keep the forests green and perpetually growing, you who love the woods will come up here to the Lake Superior country some time, no doubt, to enjoy their friendly company.

"Now wouldn't you be surprised and happy if, strolling down a woodland path on a lovely summer day, you came face to face with Paul?"

PAUL BUNYAN

When the north wind, the destroyer,
  Is loose like a fiend in the woodlands,
Stampeding among the trees,
  Spinning and driving the frozen snow,
Clutching and shaking the hardwood shanties
  Till the frail walls shriek and moan;
Then the lean, hard men of the skidway trails,
  The gray old men with gnarled hands and furrowed faces
Who heard the pine trees crash in Jim Finn's day,
  Gather in groups around the boiler stove
And tell tall yarns of vanished years.

The young men, the new men,
  The Finns and Poles and wild Hungarians,
They cluster in little bunches,
  Jabbering rapidly in their native jargons;
But the old men, the old-timers,
  The swarthy 'frog,' the nimble-fisted Irish,
The iron-fibered Scot, the blue-eyed Viking
  Gather around the stove
With visions of their youth,
  Visions of the big drives down the Menominee,
With memories of the jams on the "Blue Joe" in the Indian;
  With pungent recollections of the springtime blowouts
And hob-nails clanking along the pine-board walks—
  Of the clinking whiskey glasses
And the slattern dance-hall girls.

And ever and anon
  As they puff and spin their yarns
Their dim old eyes light up,
  And they speak of that mighty woods giant,
That hard-fisted driver of real he-men;
  That layer of lakes and builder of mountains,
That savage sawyer of pine and waster of hardwood
  That man among men who were real he-men—
The mighty Paul Bunyan!

Paul Bunyan, Paul Bunyan,
  The north wind howls in the darkness,
The mad snow snarls at the windows;
  The maples, frantic in the wild wind's clutches,
Shudder and moan and strike each other.

Paul Bunyan, greatest of loggers,
    Slasher of pine trees and waster of hardwood,
Pioneer, super-boss of Michigan's youthhood;
    Paul the mighty, where are you?
Now that the pine trees dissolve into darkness,
    And the old men, the old-timers,
The lovers of pines though they felled them and ruined them,
    Sit by the fire and dream!

Ask your bookstore salesperson for a complete listing of Avery Color Studios' Michigan and Great Lakes regional interest titles or send inquiries directly to Avery Color Studios, Star Route Box 275, AuTrain, Michigan 49806.